DEATH KNELL VI

A COLLECTION OF SHORT MYSTERIES BY DELAWARE VALLEY AUTHORS

Edited by

ELENA SANTANGELO

CONTENTS

Death Knell VI
is lovingly dedicated to the memory of

Caroline Todd

Author,
Founding member of the Delaware Valley Chapter
of Sisters in Crime,
and editor of the first four *Death Knell* short story
anthologies.

EDITOR'S NOTE

The first five *Death Knell* anthologies included notes from the editors. Notes for four of those collections were written by Caroline Todd, who was half of the writing team that produced the acclaimed Charles Todd mysteries. In the early years of the Delaware Valley Chapter of Sisters in Crime, Caroline went by her other pen name, Caroline Stafford, and not only spearheaded our first anthology project, but was a very active founder of the chapter, a prolific contributor to our newsletter, and was always willing to mentor up-and-coming writers. I learned more about editing from her than all the professional editors I've worked with over the decades.

Caroline's *Death Knell* notes said, in essence, what talented authors we have in our chapter and what wonderful stories awaited the reader within the pages of each *Death Knell*. My note will be no exception. We do have exceptionally talented authors, some names familiar from their own published novels, or from having been published in previous *Death Knells*, but also, some new fresh voices which we're delighted to introduce. Let us show you around our

Delaware Valley, from the Jersey and Delaware seashores inland to Philadelphia and the surrounding Pennsylvania counties, including historic areas like Germantown and Valley Forge. You'll find traditional and not-so-traditional mysteries, psychological suspense, tales of history, the supernatural, and even glimpses into the dark secrets of the human mind. What's not to love?

I'd like to thank our Production Manager, Amy Reade, and Jacki York for her guidance in getting this project started, plus our proofreaders: Jane Kelly, Gretchen Hall, James McCrone and, again, Amy Reade. Authors are nothing without all the people behind the scenes who make our words look good.

Elena Santangelo

A FALL TO REMEMBER

MICHAEL SHAW

$\mathcal{A}$bigail's knee bounced a thousand miles per hour as she sat in the passenger seat of Emma's Mini Cooper. Emma glanced over at her fidgeting friend and laughed. "My driving still makes you nervous after all these years?"

"It's not your driving!" Abigail laughed. "Well, not *just* your driving!"

"I'm a great driver!" Emma said with mock outrage, just before swerving to avoid something in the road.

Abigail laughed again, "Sure, you'd be a fabulous driver if we were in a demolition derby."

"One crash! In all the years I've been your own personal Uber driver, just one. And it wasn't even serious," Emma said with an exaggerated sigh. "I don't mind driving you, Abs. I just wish you didn't act like I scared you half to death."

"Only about a third to death," Abigail grinned.

"Seriously, what's got you so nervous?" Emma asked.

"You know I don't go to many parties. And this one is weird."

Emma turned the wheel hard and the Mini nearly fishtailed taking the tight curve too fast. "Not that strange. Murder mystery dinners are fun!"

"C'mon," Abigail protested, pulling her copy of the invitation from the passenger sunshade. She read aloud, "The pleasure of your company is requested on October 15 for 'A Fall to Remember,' a lavish dinner and interactive murder mystery. Cocktails and hors d'oeuvres served at 5:30 p.m., dinner promptly at 7:00 p.m., murder shortly thereafter. The first guest to unmask the murderer will be rewarded one million dollars."

"Right? Sounds exciting!" Emma said, making another hairpin turn as Abigail clenched her teeth and held her breath.

"We don't even know who our host is, and we were given coordinates, not an address. Coordinates! Who does that? Plus, our invitations were hand delivered. That doesn't weird you out?"

"It's all part of the mystery, Abs. Who doesn't love a good mystery?"

Abigail frowned. "I hate them. I have enough anxiety already, thank you very much."

"Well, I'm glad we're going. It'll be fun!"

Despite her nerves, Abigail did feel a little excited. Attending a mysterious party was something she might've done in college, but those days were long in her rearview mirror. After her freshman year, Abigail grew more reticent about trying new things. She'd become more introspective and introverted when once she'd been outgoing and impulsive. She didn't especially like this version of herself and often longed to be more like fun, impetuous college Abby than stuffy, safe, boring real-world Abigail.

"Your idea of a good time now is getting together with your book club," Emma scoffed.

"So? I like books. And wine!"

"And I like a million bucks!" Emma laughed.

WITH EMMA'S NEXT TURN, it felt as if they had been transported from Philadelphia's Delaware County suburbs to an enchanted forest. They'd been on a normal suburban street and then, suddenly, they were engulfed on both sides of the road by towering trees. Abigail had no idea what kind of trees they were, but they sure didn't seem to belong in Delco. How had she lived here her entire life and not realized such a place existed, practically in her own backyard?

Emma's GPS instructed her to make another turn. A short distance later, Abigail pointed to a tall wrought iron gate and said, "This must be the place."

Imposing granite plinths stood to either side of the gateway. Atop each, looking ready to pounce, were twin bronze lions. *They look like they're guarding against intruders,* thought Abigail, her flesh goosepimpling despite having an invitation. The gate was closed but swung open as the Mini approached. They followed an impossibly long driveway until it curved into a circle before the mansion. Emma pulled her car behind a Honda.

"Look at that," Emma said, pointing at the Civic's rear window's Widener University lion decal with the text, *Widener Pride Proud.* "A fellow member of the Pride." Emma had the same decal on her car. Abigail and Emma had first met during their freshman year at Widener. Their rooms had been across from one another in Boettner Hall, and they'd been friends from the start.

"Weird," Abigail said.

"Lots of people around here went to Widener," Emma shrugged.

They gasped as they took in their first view of the

mansion. Although still an hour before sunset, the sky had been gray all day and the impressive stone edifice was dramatically lit with strategically placed uplighting, revealing an immense English Tudor style estate. The entranceway stood beneath an impressive portico. Before they could knock, the imposing doors opened inward. A young woman, wearing a black tuxedo complete with tails and a masquerade mask that looked like a hornet, stood inside.

"Good evening," the tuxedoed woman said in a crisp voice. "You've been expected. Follow me, please. The others have already arrived."

"What's a lady butler called?" Emma asked.

"A butler," the woman replied.

"Oooh, cool. So, how many guests are there for this shindig?" Emma asked. The butler didn't reply.

They were led into a foyer with a dramatic vaulted ceiling and wood paneled walls. To their left was a wide, winding marble staircase. Abigail took in the dazzling light from a chandelier the Phantom of the Opera would kill to cut loose.

"This is a masquerade party," the butler said, explaining her mask.

"We didn't bring masks," said Abigail.

"Your masks are being provided by your host," the butler replied.

"About that," Emma said, "who is our esteemed host?"

Ignoring Emma again, the butler motioned to a table where two masks lay. The butler picked up a black and purple mask made of feathers and coal black gemstones. An obsidian beak rested over the nose. Crows had fascinated Abigail as long as she could remember. She'd even gotten a tattoo of a crow clutching her left shoulder during freshman year when she and some friends took a trip into Philly. The butler handed the mask to Abigail, as if it had been chosen especially for her. *Strange,* Abigail thought, *another Widener connection.*

The butler said, "In order to qualify for the prize, you mustn't remove your mask until instructed. You should put it on now."

The butler handed Emma the final mask, a black cat, whiskers and all, with just a touch of embellishment so it glittered when light hit it just so. Emma had snuck a black cat named Onyx into her Boettner Hall room. She'd managed to keep her hidden from the RA the entire semester. Emma hadn't gotten a cat tattoo on that Philly excursion. Hers had been a knotted Celtic cross on the back of her neck. Still, Abigail wondered if Emma's mask was more than mere coincidence.

The butler began repeating her instructions, but Emma stopped her midstream. "Got it, Jeeves. Jeevessa? Heard you the first time."

Bowing slightly the butler said, "One last instruction—guests are to address each other by their animal identity. No names, or you forfeit the contest."

"Miss Kitty," Abigail said to Emma.

With a little curtsy, Emma said, "Crowbar."

THEY WERE LED into a room large enough to accommodate an enormous wedding reception, or some other elegant gala. Another grand chandelier hung above, its many lights illuminating the room in a soft but welcoming glow. Below, a freshly waxed parquet floor looked ready to welcome revelers doing *The Electric Slide.*

To Abigail's surprise, there were only four others, all women, in the cavernous room. Emma grasped Abigail's hand and pulled her towards the others. One wore an immaculate swan mask—white feathers and golden beak, a stark contrast to Abigail's blackbird. Another looked like a doe, with a wide black nose, soft ears, and small spots of white peppered into the mask's downy brown fur. The third wore an animal Abigail couldn't identify—a mishmash lab experiment gone horribly wrong—a combination of dog, bear, raccoon, and rat, but none of those things. The final guest wore a stunning lioness mask, its fur looking like luxurious strands of gold.

"Hey, girls," Emma said as they drew close to the others. "I'm...well...I guess I'm a cat, if I want a crack at a million bucks, right? Meow!"

Abigail said, "That makes me the crow. Just one, though, so I'm not the murderer, just an attempted murder." The other guests chuckled.

"Doe," said the deer mask-wearing woman, who then sing-songed, "a deer, a female deer. Here for the dough, the cash, the cold, hard cash!" Abigail thought there was something familiar about her voice.

"Swan," said the woman wearing the white feathered mask.

"Lioness, obviously. Roar," said the golden-masked woman.

The final woman shifted uncomfortably, "I had no idea what I was. According to the butler, I'm a badger." Abigail was certain she recognized her voice.

Introductions complete, the women chatted, sipped champagne, and nibbled hors d'oeuvres. After a while, Abigail was positive she knew all but one of them. She whispered to Emma, "Have you figured out who they are?"

"Yes!" Emma said, louder than a whisper. "All but Lioness. Not sure about her."

"Me neither. Reminds me of someone, but it couldn't be

her. No doubt about the others." They'd all been Widener friends.

At precisely seven o'clock, the butler announced, "Dinner is served."

The women made their way to a table large enough for thirty, though it was set only for six. Placards rested on each plate, each with a depiction of their mask counterparts. Bowls of lobster bisque were served and while they enjoyed their soup, Swan said aloud what they'd all been thinking. "It's been a long time. Too long, but I definitely couldn't forget any of your voices. Except you," she said, glaring at Lioness. "I don't know you."

"You must be our mysterious host," alleged Badger.

Emma asked. "Why masks? And why us?"

Lioness' mouth curled up in a Cheshire cat grin. "What fun is a game without a little dress up?"

Doe asked, "So who's getting murdered?"

"I bet it's the butler," Badger said.

"Can't be. Everybody knows the butler did it!" Emma joked. "Now, where's my million?"

Just then, as if her ears were burning, the butler emerged pushing a cart with cloche-covered platers into the room. She lay one before each guest, uncovering each as she went.

"Tsk-tsk. Dinner first, then murder," Lioness chided.

"Since everybody knows everybody except you, can we at least take these stupid masks off while we eat?" Badger complained.

"Certainly," Lioness replied. "If you don't care about winning."

Conversation died down as they feasted on their sumptuous filets and lobster tails, garlic mashed potatoes, asparagus, and wine. Dessert followed—raspberry white chocolate mousse cheesecake that Doe said was to die for.

Once the butler delivered a steaming carafe of coffee, she

was dismissed and sent home. As she departed, Lioness said, "Now that we've feasted, it's time to begin our interactive murder. Follow me," she instructed. The others obeyed, stomachs satiated, but still hungry for mystery, and a chance at a million dollars.

LIONESS LED them up the marble staircase to the second floor where a railed overlook provided a grand view of the foyer below. She picked up a handgun resting on a table and cradled it like it was her child. "Now, a confession. Like any good murder mystery, this one has a twist. The murder has already been committed and one, maybe even all of you, is the killer."

"What are you talking about?" asked Doe. "What murder? Where's the victim?"

Swan rolled her eyes and said, "This is lame."

"Told you the butler was going to die," said Badger. "I'm into it. Where's her body? How'd she die?"

"Here's how this game works," Lioness said. "If one of you confesses to murder, the others go free. If one of you exposes the killer, the others go free, even though I suspect you are all complicit. If there's no confession or accusation," she said, lowering the gun at them, "then you all die."

"Is this some sort of sick joke?" Emma asked.

"Why are you doing this?" Swan demanded.

"As I'm sure you've all figured out, you each knew each other at Widener. You were friends. You did everything together. The only missing piece to the puzzle is who I am," Lioness said.

Doe asked, "Okay, who are you, then? And what did we ever do to you?"

Lioness laughed. "No, I don't expect any of you to

remember. Why would you? Everybody was disposable to you, weren't they?"

"Seriously? This is about college?" Badger scoffed. "Oh, grow up, already!"

"About college? No, it's about my life and what you took from me!" Lioness said.

"So, what, we rejected you? We embarrassed you somehow? One of us stole your boyfriend? Your girlfriend? Whatever it was, it was a decade ago. Get over it!" Badger said.

"You really don't know what I'm talking about! You have no idea," Lioness insisted.

"Then why don't you tell us?" pleaded Swan.

Emma chimed in, "Whatever you think any of us did something like ten years ago, there's got to be a better way than luring us here to murder us."

"An eye for an eye!" Lioness roared.

Something clicked in Abigail's brain. It couldn't be. It just couldn't. "Will only make the whole world blind," she replied. Gandhi's quote had been on a poster in Abby's room her freshman year. A poster that belonged to her roommate. Abigail shook her head. "You can't be who I think you are."

"Why not?" Badger asked.

"Because Benji Lawson is dead," Abigail said.

Emma's face paled and she whispered, "Benjamina?"

Lioness removed her mask and tossed it to the floor. Abigail's jaw dropped. All their jaws did. She looked exactly the way Benjamina would if she hadn't died their freshman year. "Benji? It can't be. I was at your funeral. We all were."

Then it dawned on her. Benji had a younger sister she'd told Abigail all about. She'd been so excited to follow in Benji's footsteps. What had her name been? "Georgie? Georgina Lawson, right? Benji's little sister. I remember now."

Georgie grasped at a cord, tugged, and a tapestry on the

wall behind them fell to the ground. Behind it were hundreds of photos of Benji Lawson with Abigail and the others. Smiling faces staring back at them. In each photo everyone's eyes except Benji's were cut away. "Do you remember killing my sister? Do you remember that, Abby?" Georgie asked, clutching tightly to her gun, aiming it at Abigail.

"Abby didn't kill your sister!" Swan said. "Benji's death was an accident!"

"Liar!" Georgie said, pointing the gun at Swan.

Benji had been a serious student, not interested in drinking, drugs, or boys. She hadn't cared for the silliness, as she'd put it, and wanted nothing to do with any of it. While Abby had been wild, eager to experience everything college had to offer, Benji had been…a lot like Abigail was now…shy, quiet, and bookish.

Despite their differences, they'd become friends. Abby tried including Benji whenever she hung out with her group of friends—Emma, Tish, Michele, and Sara—the four other women who'd been invited to this horror show. Sometimes Benji tagged along. Abby and Benji spent many late nights chatting in their room, sharing stories, and even a few secrets. Abby could never get Benji to go to a party, though. Not until the end of their freshman year when she finally agreed to join Abby at an off-campus party.

It had been the worst night of Abby's life, and the last night of Benji's.

Tears streamed down Abigail's face. "Georgie, I'm so sorry about Benji."

"You should be! You killed her! All of you. You're all responsible! But you're the one I blame, Abby. Benji texted me that night. She told me she was going to her first college party. She was nervous but excited. She told me it would be cool. She was going with you, and you'd make sure she had fun. You'd keep an eye out for her. Protect her. She trusted you, Abby."

"I loved your sister," Abigail pleaded. "We were friends. Please, Georgie..."

"You didn't love her enough to save her," Georgie cried.

"Fine," Abigail said. "Blame me. I deserve it. I've never forgiven myself for bringing Benji to that party. Let the others go, Georgie. If you have anyone to blame, it's me. This won't bring Benji back, though, and you know it's not what she would have wanted."

Emma stepped in front of Abigail, standing between her and Georgie. Despite clutching the gun, Georgie took a reactive step back. Emma hissed like the black cat mask she'd been wearing. "No. Abigail isn't to blame. Nobody is. What happened was tragic. An accident. The railing was rusty. Nobody could've known it would give way. Benji leaned against it, and it broke. She fell. We all saw it. Ask anybody here. They'll tell you the same thing because that's what happened. I still wake up in cold sweat dreaming about it sometimes. It was horrible, but nobody murdered her. She fell. I'm sorry she died. We all are. But it was an accident."

Abigail nodded. It had been an accident. But there was something about the way Emma explained it that sent a chill of uncertainty down her spine. It sounded so cold, so rehearsed.

It sounded like a lie.

"I don't believe you," Georgie spat, swinging the gun wildly from one woman to the next. "I've spent years dwelling on this. I've read the police reports, the statements you all gave. I've found all the inconsistencies in your stories. The contradictions. It was no accident, it was murder. One of you did it and the rest of you are covering for her. It's been one big, elaborate lie and you're all in on it. Now one of you confesses or you're all going to pay."

"It was an accident," Emma repeated forcefully.

Georgie scoffed, "Benji never would've been on a fire escape. She was terrified of heights. The only way she could've fallen is if somebody forced her out there and pushed her."

In a sudden flash of rage that caught everyone off guard, Emma lunged forward and shoved Georgie with violent force. Georgie tottered back on her heels, lost her footing, and toppled over the railing. Georgie's mouth opened wide in shock as she fell backwards, but she made no sound.

"Like that?" Emma said, ice in her voice.

Georgina Lawson lay on the granite floor, her body contorted at unnatural angles the way only a lifeless body could. Abigail glanced down and quickly turned away, sure she would throw up the canapes and raspberry-filled puff pastries she'd devoured earlier. She turned to face Emma, who stood over the railing looking down at the body. Abigail dared to look back down, only she didn't see Georgie. Abigail's vision blurred as Georgie's motionless form transformed.

Benjamina Lawson lay on the macadam, her body contorted at unnatural angles the way only a lifeless body could. Abby, Emma, Michele, Sara, and Tish looked down at the body in stunned horror from the second-floor fire escape. Moments before, Benji had been on the fire escape with them.

"Benji..." whimpered Abby, lower lip quivering, arms outstretched as if there was still a chance to grasp her roommate, her friend, bringing her back to safety.

"WHAT DID YOU DO? Emma, what did you do?" Abigail pleaded.

"I did what I had to, Abs. Georgie was going to kill you. She was going to kill us all. If she had her way, we'd all be dead," Emma said, reaching out to touch Abigail's shoulder reassuringly. "I was not going to let that happen to you. I'll always protect you, Abs."

Abigail recoiled from Emma's touch, pulling away and coming precariously close to toppling over the railing herself. "Not Georgie, Emma. *Benji.* You killed Benji. You pushed her! Emma, how could you?"

"What are you talking about, Abby? You were there. You saw it. Benji fell when the railing broke," Emma said.

Abigail screamed, "You killed her!"

"No, sweetie, you're wrong," Emma assured her. "She fell. It was an accident."

Abigail started sobbing. "No. I remember it now. I remember it all. How did I forget what really happened?"

"You remember it wrong, Abby. Benji fell," Tish said. "C'mon, think back. Remember what really happened. Locust."

"What?" Abigail asked.

"Locust, Abby," Emma said.

"Locust," Sara and Michele said simultaneously, almost in a whisper.

That word. It triggered something in Abigail's memory.

Benji stepped forward on the fire escape, losing her footing as her heel caught on the metal grate. Falling forward, reaching out, touching the railing. The railing gave way. Falling to the ground, Benji screamed as she fell. Then a crunch. And then silence.

"Do you remember now, Abs?" Emma asked. "She fell. Locust."

Benji fell. Slipped, fell, died. Abigail nodded, remembering it all.

Except there was something more. Something Emma had

omitted. It was blurry, out of focus, evading her memory. Abigail concentrated. The memory fought desperately against her, but Abigail fought back. Something came to her.

Hands, arms, pushing.

Benji had been pushed.

Abigail couldn't see who pushed Benji. Then she understood.

Benji was laughing at her. Mocking her over something stupid. Something trivial. It was so uncharacteristic of Benji. They almost never fought. Abby grew upset, angry. She screamed at Benji and backed her onto the fire escape, where the others were hanging out. Abby screamed again as she shoved Benji into the railing. The rusty railing snapped, broke, and fell to the ground below. Benji threw up her arms, trying to regain her balance, but momentum took her over. Abby tried to reach out to catch her, but she only grasped at air and Benji fell, fell, fell.

Abigail started sobbing, her mouth trembling as she processed what she'd just remembered. "B...Benji," she stammered. "I killed—"

"Shh," Emma said, touching her palm to Abigail's face. Her hands were so cold, and her touch soothed Abigail. "No, no, no. It's okay, Abs. It was an accident. You were angry. Yes, you pushed her. But the railing was rusty. You tried to grab her, to save her. You didn't mean for it to happen. We weren't going to let one little thing ruin your entire life. One mistake. One accident. Let us help you forget it again, okay? You shouldn't have to remember it. Locust, Abs."

"Locust," her college friends, her accomplices after the fact, repeated over and over again, in low, hushed voices. Emma brushed her fingers through Abigail's hair, calming her. Abigail blinked, as if coming out of a daze. Or returning to one, as the hypnotic suggestion they'd long ago employed finally took hold again.

Abby had been inconsolable after the accident, a mental

and emotional wreck. She'd wanted to confess what she'd done. She would have ruined her life, destroyed all their lives. Emma wouldn't allow it and persuaded her mother, a world renown psychologist, to help them hypnotize Abby, planting a false memory in her mind. A false memory that had worked perfectly until tonight.

Abigail stopped crying and drew a deep breath. She closed her eyes and sat in silence. Finally, she looked up at her friends.

"How are you feeling, Abby?" Sara asked.

"I have such a headache," Abigail said. "Emma, I want to go. Will you drive me home?"

Placing her arm around Abigail's shoulder, Emma led her downstairs, sure to steer her away from Georgie's crumpled body. She escorted her from the mansion, trusting the others to deal with the body. Emma helped Abigail into the Mini Cooper. As she closed the door, she whispered, "I'll always protect you, Abs."

MICHAEL SHAW WRITES about strange worlds, quirky and colorful characters, and bizarre and unusual situations, featuring elements of the inexplicable, improbable, and downright impossible. Michael is the co-founder and 2023 President of the Pitman Writers' Guild and a proud member of the Delaware Valley Chapter of Sisters in Crime. In 2021, Michael received the Leon B. Burstein / Mystery Writers of America – New York Chapter Scholarship for Mystery Writing. Originally from Springfield, Delaware County, Pennsylvania, Michael currently resides in Pitman, New Jersey with his wife, Ashley, their two dogs; Eleanor Roosevelt and Bogart, and two cats; Gatsby and Voodoo.

TWIST OF FATE

A. DIANNE READE

Something was going on and Lorna Trotter intended to find out what it was.

She and Jack had just "celebrated" their thirtieth wedding anniversary: he by allegedly working a fourteen-hour shift, she by having dinner and drinks with her best friend, Sheri. Lorna was in bed by the time Jack got home. She was awake but lay perfectly still with her eyes closed, just to see what he would do. When he joined her, he faced away from her on his side of the bed, close to the edge. So close, in fact, he was lucky he didn't end up on the floor.

Every night had been like that for the last eighteen months, when their youngest, at age twenty-three, had found a steady job and moved out of their home along the Jersey shore. Their grown-up little girl now had her own apartment in Philadelphia, making her parents empty-nesters. Lorna missed her daughter and, truth be told, was a little jealous of her. If she hadn't met Jack, Lorna could have lived in Philadelphia, too, working as a biomedical engineer.

Her engineering career seemed a lifetime ago.

When Lorna had first broached the subject of their love

life to Jack, he had replied with an exhausted sigh and reminded her (as if she could possibly have forgotten) that his plastic surgery practice was booming and he was too tired for anything else.

He had been tired ever since.

A few nights after her anniversary, Lorna met Sheri for drinks in a little place along Dune Drive in Avalon and asked the question she had been reluctant to voice for so long.

"Do you think there's another woman?"

Sheri took just a half-second too long to answer.

"You do." Lorna wasn't surprised, but she had hoped Sheri would immediately reject the idea.

"I think it's a possibility." Sheri grimaced.

Lorna looked away. The bartender was busy at the other end of the bar, but finally he glanced in Lorna's direction. She nodded and held up her index finger. He ambled over to her.

"Do you want another drink?" Lorna asked Sheri.

"No, thanks."

Lorna ordered another Foghorn. The bartender moved away to prepare it.

"Is that your third?" Sheri asked, as if she didn't know.

"Probably, but I deserve it." Lorna waved her hand with a little too much breeziness.

Sheri gave Lorna a sympathetic look, something Lorna found unbearable.

"Who could it be? The other woman, I mean." Lorna said. "My money is on his office manager, Felicity something-or-other. You should see her. She's gorgeous, she has a perfect figure, she's young. And single, no kids. She makes me sick."

"What makes you think it's her?"

"Besides her looks? Proximity. He spends more time with her than he does with me. She's the first person he sees when he gets to work and the last person he sees before he leaves the office at night. Which, incidentally, is getting later and later."

"I don't know, Lorna. Do you really think he'd go for his office manager? That would be a little too obvious, wouldn't it? Besides that, he's not dumb enough to date someone who works for him."

"That's just what makes it so brilliant. People would assume he'd never do anything so stupid and transparent, so that's exactly what he does. It's like hiding in plain sight."

"You might have a point." Sheri shrugged. "How old is she?"

"Twenty-seven. And her boobs are real. Can you believe it?"

Sheri cocked one eyebrow. "How do you know they're real?"

"Jack told me."

The bartender brought Lorna's Foghorn and she asked for the bill. When he had left with the credit card, Lorna looked up to see Sheri staring at her.

"Jack *told* you they're real?"

"Yeah. Is that weird?"

"Well, I'm not a doctor and I'm not married to one, but it seems like a strange conversation to have with a spouse. Or an employee, for that matter. Is it even legal to ask an employee if her breasts are real?"

"Jack looks at breasts all day long. They're not a big deal to him. He talks about them like I would talk about my arm. And the women in the office talk about them, too, so that's how Jack knows." Lorna twisted her mouth into a scowl. "Now that I think about it, all the women who work with Jack are pretty. The nurses, the assistants, everyone. Felicity is the prettiest, but they're all attractive. Do I even need to mention that they're all younger than me?" She leaned back with a sigh. "All those years as a stay-at-home mom, PTA volunteer, community volunteer...." Lorna rolled her eyes. "I should have kept working. Now it's too late—there's not much of a market for a middle-aged biomedical engineer on this little barrier island. But if I had a job, at least I would have something to think about besides Jack's co-workers."

Lorna had no intention of looking for a job.

"Maybe you need to find out more before you accuse Jack of having an affair with Felicity," Sheri said.

Lorna nodded absently. It wasn't just the office staff, she realized—the hospital was crawling with women, too. There were other doctors, nurses, techs, administrators, you name it. Lorna sighed. Maybe it wasn't Felicity.

The women left the restaurant and stood on the sidewalk talking for a couple minutes before going their separate ways.

"You sure you're going to be okay driving home?" Sheri asked.

"I promise." Lorna touched her nose with her right index finger, then her left index finger, as if she were taking a sobriety test.

Lorna needed more than three drinks to get drunk. She'd had a lot of practice.

She didn't want to go home just yet, knowing the house would be empty. Her stomach growled, reminding her she hadn't had anything to eat in hours.

A burger sounded good. But not just any old patty: one from MeisterBurger. There was one on Second Avenue near 95th Street, kitty-corner from Jack's office in Stone Harbor. A MeisterBurger with a large order of fries and a chocolate shake sounded good. She wondered if Felicity ever ate burgers and fries and milkshakes. Probably not.

Lorna parked along the street in front of the restaurant, where she could see both entrances to Jack's office. When she had picked up her order to-go, she settled into the driver's seat for dinner. She lowered her window just enough to hear the seagulls and smell the salt air blowing off the ocean a block to the east. Those things relaxed her—or at least they used to.

It couldn't hurt, she figured, to take note of who was coming and going at the office. Since it was just after Labor Day, the summer crowds had thinned, but there were still plenty of people around. She needn't worry about Jack noticing her in case he came out.

Because it was early evening, she figured the office staff would soon be leaving for the day. She was right.

The first one out was the pert little thing who answered the phones. Lorna couldn't remember her name, only that she was vapid. Jack *couldn't* be having an affair with her. She would bore him to death. Lorna rarely went into the office, but when she did the receptionist was always filing her nails and texting.

Right behind her came the physician's assistant. If Lorna recalled correctly, her name was Anne. Lorna's eyes narrowed. Anne was in close contact with Jack all the time— possibly as often as Felicity. She was probably in her mid-to-late forties, but she had long, lush chestnut hair that she wore swept into a ponytail. Lorna remembered when she wore her own hair that long. That was before she had kids; after kids, she cut her hair because everything just seemed easier that way. Lorna made a mental note to find out more about Anne.

She had to wait several minutes before someone else left through the back door. This time two women walked out together. Lorna recognized both nurses right away. Since meeting them a couple years back, she had referred to them as Jack's Greek chorus. She was not fond of either of them. What were their names? Oh, yes. Darcy and Deborah. Darcy, the shorter of the two, had a nasal voice that grated on Lorna's nerves. She wondered how Jack could stand it. He couldn't possibly be having a relationship with someone whose voice was so irritating, so she immediately discounted Darcy as The Other Woman. But Deborah …. she had a porcelain complexion and red hair in a pixie cut. She was definitely cute. But there was that tendency to give a running commentary on everything that went on in the office, and Lorna was pretty sure Jack would want none of that in a paramour.

Lorna counted on her fingers. Four women had come out, so Felicity would probably be next. Two women left through the front door. Patients, Lorna assumed. Jack might be a cheating reprobate, but he would never, *ever* put his medical license in jeopardy by having a romantic relationship with a patient.

The door opened and Felicity emerged from the office, walking with finely honed elegance in her high heels. Her impossibly long legs descended from a demure knee-length pencil skirt. A gorgeous chiffon blouse completed the effect. Felicity was a vision—Lorna couldn't argue with that. She turned around suddenly to talk to someone who must have been standing in the doorway. It had to be Jack. A moment later Felicity gave one of her dazzling smiles and waved. Lorna felt her stomach lurch.

Lorna was watching Felicity fold her legs into her car when a motion at the edge of the parking lot attracted her attention. It was Jack's car. She hadn't even noticed it wasn't there. She watched as he pulled into the parking spot next to Felicity. Obviously, he hadn't been the one in the doorway.

He got out of the car and Felicity rolled her window down to speak to him. There was that blinding smile again. It made Lorna sick.

Jack placed his hand on the roof of Felicity's car and tilted his head down to talk to her. Lorna wished she could hear what they were saying. After a few moments, Jack tapped the roof of her car and Felicity pulled out of her spot. He watched her leave, then opened the passenger door of his own car.

Lorna's mouth dropped open when she saw him lift a stunning bouquet of flowers in every shade of pink from the front seat. Who were those for? He hadn't even sent her flowers on their anniversary.

She felt her chest constrict as she watched him go through the back door of his office. Who could be in there?

Was it possible he was just picking up flowers to put on the reception desk?

Doubtful. He had employees who could do that for him, plus the flower shop delivered, so that wasn't the answer. Those flowers were for someone, and it was someone Jack obviously didn't want the whole office to know about. Otherwise, he would have had them delivered during business hours. And interestingly, they didn't seem to be for Felicity.

Any thought Lorna might have had about going home evaporated. She had to know who those flowers were for. Now she had no choice but to wait for Jack to leave the office and follow him.

She kept her eyes trained on the back door of Jack's office for over an hour. It was getting dark when the door finally opened.

Whoever was carrying the flowers came out first, followed closely by Jack. Lorna could only see a pair of pumps and a skirt under those huge blooms. She craned her neck as the person fumbled with something, probably a key fob, and Jack hurried to open the driver's side door of a sleek Jaguar parked a few spots away from his own car. At a word from the person holding the flowers, he opened the door behind the driver's seat. He took the flowers from the woman and as he was placing the flowers on the back seat, Lorna got a good look at her as she slid behind the wheel.

Her eyes widened. It was Dr. Spooner. Lorna had forgotten all about Dr. Spooner.

Melanie Spooner was a plastic surgeon who often worked with Jack, seeing the patients who preferred a female doctor. As Lorna recalled, Dr. Spooner worked at Jack's office two or three days a week. She must work out, Lorna thought, to have a body that good at her age. She had to be, what, fifty-two? Just a year or so younger than Lorna.

And Melanie was married.

Lorna's fists curled reflexively into tight balls of fury. They were *both* two-timing home wreckers. She was going to have to do something about this. Should she call Dr. Spooner's husband to tell him what was going on?

While she pondered this, she watched with alarm as Jack rounded the back of Melanie's car and slid into the front passenger seat. That call to Dr. Spooner's husband could wait. First things first: she needed to know where Jack and Melanie were going.

Melanie turned right out of the parking lot. Lorna started her car and gunned the engine a tad too hard as she jerked the steering wheel to pull away from MeisterBurger. She narrowly missed hitting the car parked in front of her. At the intersection of Second Avenue and 96th Street, she let two cars get between her and the Jaguar.

She followed them for miles, across the causeway and onto the mainland. The traffic was heavy, but she managed to keep them in sight while maintaining a discreet distance. She wasn't surprised when Melanie turned into the parking lot of a chic restaurant just off the main street of Cape May Court House. She and Jack had dined there, but not for years. Soft yellow lights illuminated the landscaping and the old stone building. The effect was enchanting.

Just the place for a romantic dinner for two, Lorna thought bitterly. She drove past the restaurant and then did a U-turn in the road and circled back just in time to see Jack lead Melanie by the elbow through the front door.

Should she wait? She didn't want to return to an empty house and, though she dreaded learning the truth, she was dying to know where they would go after dinner. So she waited. She parked in a spot facing Melanie's Jaguar, but a few cars down the row. She slumped low in her seat and kept her eyes trained on the door for what seemed like hours. When she saw the two of them emerge, she snapped to attention.

She followed them all the way back to the office, where Jack got into his own car. By then it was too dark to see their goodbye, which was just as well because Lorna knew it would make her sick to watch. Then, suddenly, through the windshield, she could see Jack's face bathed in blue light from his phone; the next moment her own phone buzzed with a text from him.

Have to go to hospital before coming home. Don't wait up.

Lorna's lip curled in a vicious and disbelieving sneer before she slammed the phone onto the passenger seat. *The hospital, my foot*, she thought.

She wasn't going to allow thirty years of marriage to end like this, with her being embarrassed and shamed by her own husband and his married lover.

She watched as Melanie pulled out of the parking lot, followed closely by Jack. Almost as if she were on autopilot, Lorna pulled out behind them, her thoughts churning.

Hadn't she given him the best years of her life? Hadn't she stretched dollars and food while he was in medical school? Hadn't she deprived herself of a promising career so he could follow his dream of becoming a doctor? Hadn't she raised their three kids to be successful and independent? And now that Jack was a prosperous and well-known plastic surgeon, wasn't their home the envy of all the neighbors? It was *all her*.

Once his career had taken off, *she* was the one who dragged the kids to and from every play date, soccer game, play practice, and band concert. *She* was the one who made sure their college applications were complete and submitted on time. *She* was the one who scheduled dentist appointments, volunteered for the PTA, signed Jack's name to the Christmas cards, and lined up babysitters for all their charity dinners.

Once again on the mainland, Jack veered right onto the parkway going north, Melanie signaled a left turn to take the parkway south, and Lorna had a decision to make. She didn't need to think too hard—she followed Melanie at a distance until Melanie turned down a rural road not far from Higbee Beach along the Delaware Bay. Later, Lorna couldn't explain why she did it. All she knew was that she wasn't about to let Melanie take everything from her. She didn't know what she was going to do, but she was going to do *something*.

Opportunity knocked when Melanie swung into a driveway about a half-mile down the road. A soft glow puddled around the base of a wrought iron lamppost nearby. The house was far enough from the road that it wasn't visible. Melanie got out of the car and walked toward the mailbox.

Lorna had switched off her headlights and slowed when she saw Melanie pulling into the driveway. Now she pressed lightly on the accelerator as she approached the property, toying with the idea of going faster.

Later, after everything went wrong, she would describe the feeling of her brain disengaging just before she pressed her right foot to the floor.

The thud that Melanie's body created as it made contact

with the grille of Lorna's car was surprisingly loud. It was the sound, more than anything else, that jerked Lorna back into awareness. She braked quickly and jumped out, leaving the door open and the engine purring softly. Glancing toward the thicket of trees separating the house from the road, she ran to where Melanie lay on the ground. Clearly no one had seen the incident, or they would have come running.

One look at the angle of Melanie's head was all Lorna needed. There was no way the woman had survived.

A moment later, Lorna was running back to the driver's side of the car when she noticed the dent in the grille and stopped cold. She bent to examine it more closely, her heart racing and her hands sweating. Was that blood? She would have to wipe off the blood and get that dent fixed, and soon. And not locally. She would come up with a plan to get it repaired once she got home. First she needed to get herself as far away from Melanie as possible.

She was driving a little too fast, so she forced herself to slow down as she approached the lights of West Cape May. Lorna hadn't cared which way she was going, only that she was driving away from Melanie's house. Now she was even further from home.

She pulled over to the side of the road and rolled down the front windows, gulping air. She leaned against her headrest and closed her eyes. She only allowed herself that luxury for a moment, though. She couldn't take the chance that someone had seen her near Melanie's house. She had to get away quickly.

She opened her eyes and her heart almost stopped when she saw the blue and red lights of a police cruiser pull up behind her. The blue and red lights went out for a split second, then went white. The cruiser's high beams switched on and a spotlight that could probably be seen from outer space illuminated everything in the vicinity. Lorna took a deep breath and willed herself to be calm. No one could even know yet that Melanie was dead, right?

Then she recalled the dented grille with a jolt. A sheen of sweat broke out across her forehead. Would the cop look at the front of the car? Her breathing became the slightest bit ragged.

A police officer wielding a flashlight walked up to the passenger window, peering into the cargo bay and the back seat as he approached.

"Everything all right, ma'am?" he asked.

"Yes, officer. I just felt a little queasy, so I pulled over."

"Feeling better now?"

"Yes." Lorna nodded.

"Would you like me to call the paramedics?"

"No, no. I'll be fine."

"Have you had anything to drink tonight?"

"No, sir." Anyway, it had been hours ago.

"Are you diabetic?"

"No."

"Does this happen often?"

"No."

"Do you have any idea what might be causing you to be sick?"

"I had a burger for dinner. It was probably that."

"Are you going to be able to get home all right?"

"Yes, sir. I'll be okay."

"As long as you're sure. I don't want to have to respond to a call saying you've hit a tree two miles up the road because you were too sick to drive."

"Don't worry. I'll get home all right."

"Take care of yourself."

"I will." Lorna nodded.

The officer stared at her for a moment, eyes narrowed, and returned to his car. Lorna eased slowly back onto the road and drove away. That had been a little too close for comfort.

When she got back to Avalon, Jack wasn't home yet. *No surprise,* she thought.

She was getting ready for bed when she heard him pull into the garage. He trudged up the stairs to the second floor, his footfalls shuffling on the carpet. When he walked into their bedroom, Lorna was toweling off her face. The sweat on her face might be gone, but her heart refused to slow down. She saw in the bathroom mirror how flushed she looked.

"Where were you all evening?" She tried to sound nonchalant.

"I had a going-away party for Melanie Spooner—she's leaving the practice. Then I had to stop at the hospital to speak to Dr. Moss, the anesthesiologist who helped out on one of my cases yesterday." Lorna recalled meeting Dr. Moss, whom Jack had invited to the office holiday party the previous year.

"I'm exhausted." Jack went into the bathroom to change into his pajamas, something he always did now. He used to change right in front of her. When he returned, he got into bed. "G'night." He turned toward the wall.

"G'night."

How's he going to react when he hears the news about Melanie?

Lorna didn't sleep well that night, what with her rib cage expanding and contracting at a rapid rate and that thudding sound playing over and over again in her mind. When she finally got up around five, the first thing she did was turn the radio on to hear the local news. Jack stirred.

There it was. The story of an as-yet-unnamed but well-respected plastic surgeon, killed in a hit-and-run last night outside her secluded home near Higbee Beach. Police were still investigating.

"Melanie lives near Higbee Beach," he mumbled. He reached for his phone on the bedside table and Lorna watched as his eyes grew wide with shock.

"My God," he breathed. "It was her. The woman they're talking about on the radio. She's dead. I've got a dozen texts about it." He closed his eyes and rubbed the bridge of his nose. Lorna wondered how he was managing to sit there without losing his mind right in front of her.

"Wow. That's too bad," she said.

Jack gave no sign of having heard her. He went into the bathroom while Lorna went downstairs to make coffee.

When he came down just a few minutes later, his hair was still wet and he was in a hurry. "I don't know when I'll be home." He left without another word.

Lorna found that she didn't want to be in the house alone that morning. She couldn't drive her car until she had it repaired, preferably in Delaware, so she biked to the gym, where she and Sheri walked on the treadmills before hitting the sauna. Lorna felt vaguely nauseous, though, and had to get out of the sauna before she threw up.

Sheri had plans, so Lorna rode into Stone Harbor for an iced coffee. She was sitting at a tiny table in the front window of her favorite coffee shop when she saw Jack drive by. Why wasn't he at the office? She wouldn't even have noticed him, but he created a bit of a scene when he screeched to a halt to avoid hitting a man in the crosswalk. The guy flipped Jack off and kept walking. Jack hung his head for a moment before proceeding slowly. If Lorna hadn't known he was upset over the death of his mistress, she would have felt sorry for him.

As she watched, Jack turned left off 96th Street and came to a stop in front of the expensive new condo complex on Third Avenue. He jogged up to the front of the building, pressed a buzzer, and waited. When no one answered the door, he pulled out his phone and texted furiously for a few moments.

As Lorna watched, Jack put the phone in his jacket pocket and walked away quickly, disappearing down the sidewalk around the south end of the complex. Lorna stood up and was about to follow him when she heard a voice say, "Mrs. Trotter?"

Lorna spun around to see Anne, Jack's PA. Anne's eye makeup was smudged and the whites of her eyes were bloodshot.

"Hi, Anne." Lorna tried to get past her so she could see what Jack was doing, but the coffee shop was so darned small. She was trapped.

"Can you believe what happened to Melanie?" Anne asked with a sniffle. "And to think we were all at her going-away party last night. And poor Jack. He's devastated. Melanie left the party early to drive him back to the office because he had to meet with Dr. Moss at the hospital. Jack feels like Melanie might still be alive if she had just stayed at the party. He's wrong, of course, but he's not listening to reason."

Lorna's breath caught in her throat for just a moment, then she nodded and put on her saddest look. "It's shocking. I'm sorry, Anne. I just can't bear to talk about it right now."

Anne nodded with understanding and stepped aside so Lorna could leave. Once outdoors, Lorna crossed the street and walked toward Third Avenue, taking care to stay close to the storefronts, mingling with the tourists. She followed the sidewalk where Jack had gone, but she didn't see him. Glancing behind her, she walked up the beautifully land-scaped path curving around behind the condos.

The back of the condo complex boasted a serene garden space surrounded on three sides by a covered colonnade. There he was. Jack was walking away from her toward someone standing at the end of one of the walkways. As

Lorna watched from a deep shadow alongside a colonnade, Jack hurled himself into the waiting arms of Dr. Moss, the anesthesiologist. They shared a long, lingering kiss while Lorna's insides twisted and squirmed.

She was so sure it had been Melanie. And if not her, then certainly the stunning Felicity.

Or .... well, anyone but Eric Moss.

Lorna stared, backing away quietly and as quickly as she dared. She had to go somewhere to think. As she emerged onto the sidewalk, a police cruiser rolled to a stop behind Jack's car. She froze for a moment, then turned around and walked quickly back toward the colonnade. To her great dismay, Jack and Dr. Moss were walking directly toward her, and this time there was nowhere to hide. She spun around again, debating whether she dared go back toward the police officer.

"Lorna?" Jack called. There was an unmistakable puzzlement in his voice, as well as a tinge of resignation at finding her there. At learning his secret. She stopped and turned to face him, her heart threatening to beat out of her chest.

"Dr. Trotter?" the officer asked, coming up behind Lorna.

"Yes." Jack looked confused.

"We're looking for your wife."

Jack gestured toward Lorna. "This is my wife. Why are you looking for her?"

Lorna closed her eyes.

The officer didn't answer Jack, but looked sternly at Lorna as he reached for the handcuffs on his belt.

"Mrs. Trotter, you're under arrest for the murder of Melanie Spooner. You have the right to remain silent...."

"What?" Jack cried. "Lorna didn't kill Melanie."

"A security camera at the Spooner residence captured the entire thing, Doctor. And an officer remembers talking to your wife near the scene of the murder last night."

Jack looked at Lorna. His expression was a mixture of disbelief, puzzlement, shock, and rage.

Jack stared at Lorna until she broke the silence. "You could have told me, you know. I would have understood. I would have forgiven anything but another woman."

A. Dianne Reade is a pen name of author Amy M. Reade, a *USA Today* and *Wall Street Journal* bestselling author of cozy, historical, and Gothic mysteries.

A former practicing attorney, Amy discovered a passion for fiction writing and has never looked back. She has so far penned three standalone Gothic mysteries, the Malice series of Gothic novels, the Juniper Junction Holiday Cozy Mystery series, the Libraries of the World Mystery Series, and the Cape May Historical Mystery Collection. In addition to writing, she loves to read, cook, and travel. Amy lives in New Jersey and is a member of Sisters in Crime and the Alliance of Independent Authors.

You can find out more and follow her on social media by visiting her website at www.amymreade.com.

GINSENG TEA

ELENA SANTANGELO

y heart near beat its way right up outta my throat. I was that scared. The ride was fine, though. First time I'd been on a horse, my family being too poor to own one. The reason for the ride, now, that was a different matter. I was a prisoner of war.

My name's Jem Freeman and, nigh as anyone can figure, I was born eleven years ago. Born to trouble, Ma always said, being female and a free Negro in a world not inclined to favor either, despite all the high and mighty talk of late from Mr. Jefferson and such. He and I share the same tendency to speak our minds, but all it ever gets me is a switch across my nether side.

Or in my present predicament, likely a hanging.

My capture was truly exciting. First, a man in a tattered brown coat grabbed my shoulder. He let go right quick when my teeth met his flesh. The name that escaped his lips wasn't mannerly, but I've been called worse. I tarried just long enough to make sure his other hand didn't hold a musket at the ready.

Old Brown Coat shouted an order and another soldier,

skinny as an eel, gave chase. As we crossed the creek, he must have slipped on the ice-covered rocks because I heard a splash followed by him swearing an oath.

A third soldier—so big and broad I knew how David felt facing Goliath—blocked my way to the road. I parried, keeping out of his arms' reach, me being more nimble than he was.

That's when I'd heard a horse behind me, and more shouts. Shouldn't have looked back. The muddy ruts in the road done me in. Could'a gotten away otherwise. If there'd been an away to get to.

Four days previous, the army had marched into Valley Forge, and the way they'd commenced to building huts, like a swarm of beavers, you could tell they planned to stay a while. I couldn't hide out all winter.

Now the mount beneath me slowed and its master hopped down, lifting me off after him. We were in front of two large tents, each bigger than the cabin I call home. Men in long cloaks stood around an open fire, talking, pointing to papers they held, their faces grim. My four escorts compared poorly to them.

Brown Coat looked more like a farmer in his dark trousers and buckskin moccasins. Under his floppy hat, his face was red and chapped by the cold. He kept his hands tucked inside his coat for warmth.

Goliath was dressed in shabby homespun. Hay was stuffed into his shoes, which looked like they'd fall apart if you breathed on them. He used his musket like a cane, so I reckoned his feet hurt.

The Eel wore a moth-eaten uniform jacket, brown with red trim, over a faded blue gingham shirt. His legs were bare from his knee breeches to his shin-high boots. One of those boots had little ice flakes all over from its sojourn in the creek.

Only the horseman looked like a genuine soldier, with his blue and white uniform, black hat, and boots that reached his knees. He was young and comely, and though muddy from running me to earth, he'd done his best to tidy himself up again.

The men around the fire seemed better off. Like the horse soldier, they all wore boots, had the same blue uniforms under their cloaks. One man in the center of the group caught my attention, the tallest, most troubled-looking of them all. His hair was a mixture of red and grey, and his voice was gentle. The way the other men treated him, I knew he must be pretty important. A general, maybe.

I laughed at my own thoughts. They wouldn't bring a poor girl like me before a general. At any rate, he was an officer.

The horse soldier approached him respectfully. "I thought you should see this, sir." He took a scrap of paper from his vest pocket and handed it over.

The officer read it and frowned. "Explain."

"The girl had it, sir. She was running from those three soldiers."

"Bring them into my marquee, Lieutenant."

I would have preferred to stay near the fire. The tent was cold, December's winds blowing right through the cloth roof, stirring up maps and such on a table in the center.

The officer settled himself on a stool, pulling his cloak around his legs. "Who will begin?"

I opened my mouth to speak, but Brown Coat stepped forward and saluted. "Sergeant Noah Magee, Ninth Pennsylvania, sir. I found this girl around the ruins of the forge. Appeared to be stealing from Colonel Dewees' iron works so, remembering your orders, sir, I tried to stop her. She bit me and ran away."

"What were you doing there yourself, Sergeant?"

"Well, sir. General Conway sent me to find him a house where he could set up his headquarters. I was on my way to ask at the farms west of here when I came on this girl. She had something in her hand, so I yelled to this soldier here and he gave chase."

The Eel stepped forward and saluted nervously. "Enoch Taylor, your Excellency. I'm a gunner, sir, Cranc's Artillery. The sergeant's telling the truth, only I didn't give chase for long. There was ice on the rocks, you see, and..." He looked down at his wet boot as if he'd committed treason.

"What were you doing down by the creek, Gunner?"

"Fetching water for my squad, your Excellency."

The officer turned to Goliath. The big soldier grinned broadly and snapped to attention, saying, "Chen'ral Vashing-don, zir!"

General Washington? You could'a blown me over. This man *couldn't* be the famous George Washington—Ma said he was ten foot tall and had a golden aura around his head. But the officer didn't deny the label, nor did he seem to mind my staring more than was polite.

Goliath pulled a much-handled sheet of paper from his under his shirt and gave it to the lieutenant who read it aloud. "It's an old pass. Private Taddeus Golinko. Second New York Regiment. At the bottom someone wrote that he's from Poland and doesn't speak English."

Private Golinko nodded his head several times, his smile broadening. General Washington asked him why he was down by the creek and what he'd seen, but Goliath just kept grinning and nodding.

The general turned his careworn gaze on me, but addressed the horseman. "Who does she belong to, Lieutenant?"

"No one, sir. I mean, she's not a slave. Her family is freeborn."

"I see. And what is her name?"

That's when I spoke, being the only one who knew the answer. "I'm Jem Freeman, sir."

General Washington seemed surprised that I had a voice. "Where do you live, Mistress Freeman?"

Having never been called 'Mistress Freeman' by anyone, I presumed myself to be in more trouble than first imagined. "Up on t'other side of Mount Joy."

"The hut you asked about yesterday, sir," the lieutenant said.

"The collier's hut? Your father's a collier?"

"Pa died of smallpox three years back. Him and my baby sister." A lump clogged up my throat, coaxing me to pause for a swallow. "My brother works for the collier, chopping wood to make the charcoal. Did, anyway, a'fore the forge got burnt. There's no call for charcoal here'bouts now."

"So you and your brother—and your mother?—live in that tiny hut?"

I felt my face flame up, imagining the kind of grand house General Washington owned. You'll excuse my words being on the proud side. "It's plenty big enough for us."

He looked me up and down, frowning. I'd been inspected in such a way by white folk before. Like they was judging livestock. "Mistress Freeman, do you know what accusations these gentlemen are making against you?"

"Don't know if I'd call *any* of them gentleman, General. 'Cept that one." I gave a nod to the lieutenant. "Seems to me, if this army's supposed to be protecting native-born Americans like myself, I got cause to worry."

The corners of the general's mouth twitched. "What were you doing at the forge, Mistress Freeman?"

"Not stealing, no sir. I was hunting up ginseng root. Miz Hewes—she lives in Mr. Potts' house down by the river—Miz Hewes took herself sick and asked Ma to make her up a tonic. Folks here'bouts is always asking Ma for tonics, and help with birthing and such. 'Any rate, Ma says Miz Hewes got herself upset 'cause the army's here. And ginseng root makes a nice, soothing tea, good for worries. I remembered seeing a patch of ginseng down by the forge last September, a'fore the British come through and burned everything. I was looking to see if the roots was still there."

General Washington held up the scrap of paper. "Where did you get this?"

"Right there by the forge, a-lying on the ground, dry and fresh-looking, like somebody just dropped it. I picked it up to have a look. That's when the sergeant grabbed my arm."

"Why did you run?"

"Begging your pardon, General sir, but maybe you don't know much about being a girl. 'Specially when there's a few thousand strange men camping 'round your home."

He turned to the horseman. "Lieutenant, what can you add?"

The soldier shook his head. "Very little, sir. I was returning from my errand to General Knox when I heard shouting. I urged my horse on but, by the time I arrived, this girl had already gained the road. I dismounted and caught her, and when I read the note she held, I knew this to be more than a case of simple thievery."

This last commenced my heart to thumping hard again. If I wasn't being accused of stealing, what did they suspect? "Begging your pardon again, General, but what exactly does that paper say?"

General Washington looked from face to face before replying. "A patrol was sent out from camp yesterday. This note details their numbers, arms, and destination. If it fell into British hands, it could mean death to every man in that detachment."

Goliath grinned and nodded. The other three turned

their accusing eyes in my direction. On the Eel's face, I saw surprise. On Brown Coat's, anger. The lieutenant looked thoughtful.

I stared right back at them. I decided then and there General Washington deserved the benefit of my sage advice. "Your Excellency, sir, I need to talk to you in private."

The general raised his eyebrows, but said, "Gentlemen, please wait outside by the fire. And dry your boot, Mr. Taylor. We can't afford more sick men."

The gunner meekly agreed and all but the lieutenant left the tent. "Him, too," I insisted.

"Lieutenant Mills is a member of my staff, Mistress Freeman. He will stay."

I gave in. You can only win so many battles. "Way I see it, you think I'm a spy." I peeked at the general, hoping for a reaction. There was none. His face was still as a piece of pink Mount Joy quartz. "I figure it's in my best interest to find the real spy for you."

"How do you propose to do that?"

"Take that paper, for instance. It never got the chance to soak up the damp from the ground. My idea is, the person who dropped it couldn't have gone far a'fore I picked it up. Only those three soldiers and Lieutenant Mills here had the chance."

General Washington turned to the younger man. "What do you think, Lieutenant?"

"I apparently have a higher opinion of Mistress Freeman than she does of me. I don't think she's our spy. Her family lost too much at the hands of the British to remain loyal to England."

"Never felt much of an attachment," I admitted, "even a'fore they burned the forge. Isn't a day goes by my brother, Asher, doesn't talk of 'listing in the army. Would'a already, if it weren't for Ma and me being left alone. As for that paper,

Lieutenant, I know you didn't drop it. There's only one person who could'a."

General Washington leaned forward, curious. "Explain, please."

"Comes back to that note. Why write down the information? You'd think a spy would keep it in his head. 'Less he couldn't deliver the message in person so he had to write it down."

"One of those three men is a courier?" the general mused. "One who can't read. If he knew what the note said, he could have memorized it and not carried the paper. And perhaps that's why he was chosen, so he wouldn't be privy to the information he bore."

"The rest is simple," I said. "The messenger was going to meet someone. Another courier, I'll wager, maybe a Redcoat. Now, if I was sneaking away from camp, I wouldn't wear a uniform. I wouldn't want to look like a soldier."

General Washington sighed. "Unfortunately, many of my men don't look like soldiers. They're lucky to have any clothes at all, let alone uniforms. If you're correct, Mistress Freeman, we can eliminate Mr. Taylor, but two remain."

"Private Golinko," Lieutenant Mills suggested. "He can't speak English, let alone read it. Even if our sentries questioned him as he left camp, they'd lose their patience soon enough."

I shook my head. "The private's shoes were falling off his feet. I doubt he could'a walked more than a few miles. If I was that spy, I'd make sure my messenger wore a good pair of shoes."

The general stroked his chin. "Lieutenant, bring Sergeant Magee back in."

Directly accused, Brown Coat confessed at once. "I was only following orders, sir. General Conway was sending that note to General Gates in York, to keep him and Congress informed—"

"I send Congress my own reports, Sergeant."

"Yes, sir. But General Conway ordered me. I didn't know what was on the paper. Only that I was to meet a man in a canoe up where Perkiomen Creek meets the Schuylkill River."

General Washington inhaled angrily. "You may go, Mistress Freeman. Thank you for your help. Lieutenant Mills, take her to her house."

I FOUND myself once more seated in front of the lieutenant on his horse, enjoying my second ride of a lifetime. "What'll happen to Sergeant Magee?"

"Not much." Lieutenant Mills snapped the reins to urge his horse up the hill. "He was following orders and General Conway will back him up. The army's supplies are long overdue and their pay is three months behind. General Washington can't afford to be hard on anyone right now."

"What'd the sergeant mean, about General Gates?"

"Some people think General Gates would be a better Commander-in-Chief. They're doing everything they can to have General Washington replaced."

"This General Conway's one of them?"

I could tell the lieutenant was frustrated by how his hands tightened on the reins. "General Conway has given General Washington a particularly difficult time."

I mulled that over. "This General Gates, how's he any better than General Washington?"

"Some say we're not winning more battles because of a lack of training. The Lobsterbacks are professional soldiers, after all, and we're merely volunteers. General Gates has fought wars in Europe. Some say he knows more about the subject." Lieutenant Mills didn't sound convinced.

"You like General Washington better?"

"That I do, Mistress. He cares *why* we're fighting and doesn't let the army forget it. He won't give up, no matter how bad things get."

I knew all about things getting bad. The war had seemed far away last year, just stories told by the teamsters come out of Philadelphia. My Quaker neighbors had talked of peace.

Now I gazed out over their fields, remembering how they'd appeared in late summer, full of the promise of a good harvest. Instead, the crops had been scavenged and trampled by the Redcoats, leaving precious little to share with the thousands now camped here, building huts in those same fields. Chopping down most of the trees. Churning the soil into foul soup.

Now the talk wasn't of peace, but of whether there were provisions enough to get through winter. If there'd be a spring planting. If Mr. Potts and Colonel Dewees would rebuild the Mount Joy Iron Works, so's my brother could earn some pay again.

One other thought was on my mind. "I guess General Washington... I guess he own a passel of black slaves, don't he?"

I saw the lieutenant's gloved hands tighten on his reins. "Yes, he does. In fact, two of them will be joining him here soon, to see to his needs while we're encamped."

Strange, I thought, how high and mighty people seem to need poor folk to care for them, as if their money makes them forget how to do for theyselves. Even if hard times were coming this winter, my family knew how to hunt and fish and find plants to eat, and our little home, build partly into the south side of Mount Joy, could be kept warm enough.

This last thought reminded me to ask the lieutenant to let me off while we were still out of sight of the cabin. "Ma sees me riding up with you she's like to die of fright."

He obliged, dismounting and lifting me to the ground once more. "Thank you for your help, Mistress Freeman."

"You don't have slaves, do you, sir?"

"No, Mistress."

"Didn't think so. You don't look at me the same way."

Lieutenant Mills removed half a beechnut bur from his steed's mane. "My father came to this country as an indentured servant when he was a boy. He worked hard for a cruel master for seven years. When he should have been given his freedom, the master used trickery and legally bound him on another two terms." Standing straighter, the horseman added, "My father won't have his children hold servants in that fashion, indentured or slave. And I agree with him."

"Well, Lieutenant, while the army's here, you'd be welcome in our home any time."

He swept off his hat and bowed low. "That would be my honor, Mistress."

I tried to do a proper curtsy in response, just the way I seen Miz Hewes do when her preacher come to call.

The lieutenant swung back into his saddle. "Mistress Freeman, if you find any of that ginseng root, I'd be pleased to buy some of the tea mixture from your mother. I could use something warm and soothing for the cold nights ahead."

"You leave it to me, sir. Even if I can't find the ginseng, I'll bring you something good."

He smiled. "I'd like that fine, Mistress." And touching his hat to me, he rode off.

ELENA SANTANGELO IS the author of 7 novels in the Twins Mystery Series and the Possessed Mystery Series, including BY BLOOD POSSESSED, which was nominated for an Agatha Award. Her armchair companion to Agatha Christie's short stories, DAME AGATHA'S SHORTS, won the Agatha for Best Nonfiction. She's also published numerous short stories, and co-edited six anthologies of short fiction. She's a proud founding member of Delaware Valley Sisters in Crime. A version of "Ginseng Tea" was first published in Potpourri Magazine and won the National Council for Literature's Award for Fiction for a children's story.

THE CHILDREN WILL LEAD US

NANCY BIALY DAVERSA

Marcin Manor, Bucks County, Pennsylvania — 1938

"Yeah, over here with the body," replied Lieutenant Bailey. He was dressed in the famous trench coat he wore during World War I. He was looking at something he had never seen before.

The hole was in the man's neck, under the jawbone near the ear where the carotid artery was torn. It was not round like from a bullet or straight across from a knife wound. Lieutenant Bailey told Corporal Harlan, the newest police officer on the force, "There was a time when a cop would put his finger in the hole to judge the distance that the bullet came from or how deep a knife wound was, but not now, what with blood diseases and all, we leave that for the medical examiner to answer." Bailey never mentioned his age, but being in World War I meant he was in his late thirties.

The Marcin mansion had a view of the Delaware River right out the front door. It was in the richest area of Bucks

County, especially on North Park Lane where these people lived.

Mr. Marcin, the mansion owner, stood with Lieutenant Bailey over the body in the servant's quarters on the estate property. He was in his forties and dressed like a very rich man.

Mr. Marcin looked down at the victim and sighed, "Poor old Duffy. He was the best groundskeeper we ever had." Then he began to shake his head.

Lieutenant Bailey looked from Corporal Harlan to Mr. Marcin then said, "The hole is not round. It has odd jagged, serrated markings, like in the last two animal deaths on these grounds that we got called out on during the last couple of weeks."

"What exactly is this place?" Corporal Harlan asked.

"It's an old mansion on prime real estate." Mr. Marcin answered with his head held high.

"That's seen better days," Corporal Harlan said under his breath.

"I wonder why the groundskeeper had his gun near him, and didn't use it?" Lieutenant Bailey was thinking aloud.

"The monster," said a little girl, who had quietly entered the area between them and the house on the hill. Lieutenant Bailey wondered if she was calling the dead man a monster or the murderer?

"Sissy, get out of here!" Mr. Marcin commanded, "And where is Joey?"

"In his room, Father."

"Well, go play a game with him."

Sissy refused to move.

Mr. Marcin turned back to the officers. "Sorry for the interruption. She's nine going on twenty-one."

"All right. But she said something about a monster?" Bailey mentioned.

"That's why our groundskeeper had the gun near him. Something's been killing our animals," Mr. Marcin stated.

"We know, the police have been called about the animals recently. What do you think it is?" Corporal Harlan asked with his notebook opened and pen in hand, all set to take notes. There was a rumor about Harlan that he must sleep in his car because his clothes were usually wrinkled. He was twenty-three with blue eyes and blonde-streaked hair. Never talked about dating. Everyone wondered why.

"Don't know, but they all seem to have marks like on our groundskeeper's neck." Mr. Marcin stated.

"Do you think the murderer has stepped up his game? You know, maybe now he's not getting satisfaction with killing animals?" Mr. Marcin suggested.

At that moment, his wife appeared. Mrs. Marcin looked like a cover girl on one of the famous magazines. She presented the medical examiner, Dr. Joseph Hughes. She had been asked by another officer to wait in front of the mansion for the medical examiner and to lead the man to the servant quarters.

Moments later the medical examiner, who looked more like an accountant, came out of the servant quarters and walked over to where the homeowners and lieutenant were standing. He told the group that it looked suspicious to him, but the exact results would have to wait until the autopsy was completed.

The officers searched the area while the police photographer was busy shooting the scene. Other officers were taking measurements before the paramedics' removal of the body. The Lieutenant and Corporal walked the Marcins back to the main house to start interviews of those living on the grounds.

As they were walking toward the house, Lieutenant

Bailey asked the Marcins, "How many children do you have, and who else is here?"

Mr. Marcin answered a little out of breath once they were halfway up the hill to the house. Corporal Harlan started taking more notes. "We have two children. Sissy, age ten -- you saw her running around outside -- and her younger brother, Joey, who is eight. There is the day cook and house-keeper, Tamara, but she called in sick today. And then Grand, my wife's mother and her sister, Aunt Irene, who are down from Connecticut for a two-week vacation."

Sissy ran up to the Georgian style house but turned and took the sidewalk to enter it through another doorway.

Just before entering the house through the main doorway, Mrs. Marcin tapped her husband on the arm and said, "Don't forget Hunter was here last night. He was a bit, how shall we say, in his cups and unable to drive back to his place."

"You mean he was in a drunken stupor. I saw him when he came in," said Mr. Marcin. He then walked over to the window in the parlor, looked out and said, "Hunter's car is gone."

Lieutenant Bailey asked, "Who is Hunter?" Sounding a bit out of breath as he also was walking up the hill to the home.

Mrs. Marcin stated, "My husband's son from his first marriage. He is nineteen but looks about twelve and is a college student at Princeton University. He is dealing with a BA degree in mental health."

Corporal Harlan's pencil broke. He fished into his coat pocket for another.

Lieutenant Bailey demanded the couple contact Hunter to return to the estate immediately.

All looked up in time to see the little girl hanging out her second floor bedroom window.

Mr. Marcin yelled for her to stop leaning out the window and close it. Which she did quickly.

All walked inside. Mr. Marcin excused himself to go into his library and contact Hunter.

On the second ring, Mr. Marcin was heard to say, "Hey, it's your father. There is a bit of trouble here at the house. Could you please get back as soon as possible?"

Just then there was a scream coming from the direction of the kitchen. Once by the kitchen door, Harlan saw another concern, While going out the kitchen back door to retrieve some garden vegetables, the cook nearly slid on a rabbit, that had been killed by someone in the same manner as the groundskeeper, and then the animal carcass seemed to have been dragged across the back doorway.

"Have everyone in the family come into the parlor," Lieutenant Bailey turned to Corporal Harlan, "Go find the medical examiner and tell him to collect and examine the dead rabbit for forensic evidence."

"You surely don't want the children in the parlor?" Mrs. Marcin asked, starting to look a bit frenzied.

"Of course not, only the adults, this is a serious matter." Lieutenant Bailey replied.

Corporal Harlan left to talk to the medical examiner.

Minutes later, Hunter came through the front door, then into the parlor. He placed a box on the parlor coffee table with napkins. After taking a donut and his seat on the couch, Hunter began asking what was happening at the back door and near the servant's quarters. Aunt Irene, the purple-haired one and Grand with her penciled in eyebrows and strong smell of a vapor rub, sat on either side of him looking at the box of donuts. He nodded for them to pick their own.

Lieutenant Bailey started, "Now I am not sure of what is going on here, but I intend to find the underlying cause of this. Let us start with you, Hunter. Last name please."

"Hughes, and before you ask, I live in the apartment over the carriage house about a mile from here."

"Where did you go this morning?" The Lieutenant asked.

"To the store to get donuts for the family." Hunter's voice was soft, possibly due to his hangover. "I do it every Saturday morning."

"Where?" Corporal Harlan asked as he looked down at the donuts, then said, "I see Lotto's written on the box. That's just down the road. How long were you gone?"

"Two hours," Sissy said, sitting next to her brother, swinging her feet between the railings on the second-floor balcony that overlooked the Foyer and Parlor.

"How did you know this?" Sergeant Harlan called up to her.

"My favorite cartoon show had just started when I saw him leave the house. It always starts at 8 a.m."

Mr. Marcin rose and said, "Thank you for your information, now please go to your room. This is adult business."

Sissy turned to her brother and said, "Shall we try to solve it before they do? We don't need them. We are smarter than adults. We can figure it out way before they do." She said this just loud enough for the adults below to hear.

Corporal Harlan left the room but returned shortly, He told the Lieutenant, "The medical examiner is nearly finished. Mind if I ask a few questions?" Bailey nodded.

Harlan turned to Hunter and said, "So, you were gone two hours to pick up donuts. Where else did you go?"

"Oh, I forgot. Grand over there asked me to pick up her prescription. She was supposed to call it in, but when I got to the pharmacist, he said no phone call was received. I called back here and reminded Grand about the pills. She had me give the pharmacist the phone, she told him what she needed, and then I waited for the prescription to be filled."

"Where are my pills?" Grand asked.

Hunter looked into the bag with the napkins and fished around. "Guess they're still in the car."

Grand got up and said she was going to retrieve her medicine from Hunter's car and promised to be right back. She took Hunter's keys off the coffee table and left.

Lieutenant Bailey turned to Aunt Irene and asked, "What have you been up to these last twenty-four hours?"

Irene was flustered at the question. She blushed and began shaking. "Nothing, just in my room reading a murder mystery."

"Got any ideas of what is going on here?" Bailey continued.

"This is no laughing matter, officer. Any one of us could be next. All I can say is it's a good thing Henry didn't come with me this time." Aunt Irene stated.

"And Henry is?"

"My blue heeler."

"You come with medical personnel every time you travel?" He could not believe it, she seemed so normal.

"No officer, a blue heeler is a breed of dog."

"Did not know that." Bailey smiled at her. She returned the smile.

The Lieutenant could hear the children on the second floor, whispering to each other in low voices. Sissy turned to Joey, who was holding two of the stairway spindles in the railing, with his head between them looking down at the adults. Sissy was too big to do this, but she still planted herself on the floor next to her brother with an unobstructed view down into the Parlor.

She said, "Joey."

"Yes?"

"Want to try and solve this mystery?"

Joey replied, "Not really. I'm going back in my room to play with my marbles."

"Oh, come on, it'll be fun."

"No thanks," he said and then started to rise. "I like action things. This is boring. Just a bunch of old people talking." Joey rose and left. Sissy continued to listen to the adult conversations below. "I guess I read too many murder mysteries, but this one fascinates me," she said aloud to herself.

"Hey, you up there, please leave, this is for adults only," the Lieutenant called up to Sissy.

"I don't have to," Sissy whined but rose.

"Yes, you do," her father called up to her.

"But I don't want to."

"Want a ride in a police car for interrupting an investigation?" Corporal Harlan said under his breath as he was walking closer to the staircase where the little girl was.

Sissy's mother broke in, "This is quite enough." She turned toward her daughter and said, "Sissy, get to your room, this instant. Close the door and keep it that way until I come up and get you."

"All right Mother." Sissy said and stomped off down the second-floor hallway. Moments later a door slammed.

"Okay, everyone, back to the business at hand," Lieutenant Bailey stated. Turning to Aunt Irene, he asked, "So you two came here for two weeks."

"Ten days," Aunt Irene answered while pulling at her sweater.

"Fine, have you heard or seen anything, let's say, unusual?" he asked.

She shook her head.

Then he said, "Are you sure?"

She thought for a moment and then replied, "Nothing out of the ordinary."

"You want to take a minute to think about it before you answer?" Lieutenant Bailey asked.

"No, thank you," Aunt Irene replied quickly.

Bailey took another approach. "Where do you live?"

"We're retired and Grand and I live together in a retirement community called Hershey's Run, in Farmington, Connecticut."

"Do you feel these people can keep you safe if something else happens?" Bailey pointed to the Marcins.

"Yes," she said and smiled.

"Thank you." The Lieutenant finished with her. He had already interviewed the Marcins in the servant's quarters and concluded that they were innocent. So, Hunter and Grand were the only ones left to question. While the Lieutenant was about to speak, Grand returned from retrieving her prescription from the car. In her hands, besides her pills, was a bloody hammer.

"Lieutenant, I bet this is the murder weapon?" she stammered and held it up for all to see.

"Where did you find it?"

"Inside the car."

"You shouldn't have taken it from the car," Bailey reprimanded her.

She sat down and said, "Sorry but I got so excited about finding it. It's the murder weapon, right?"

"That's ridiculous, Grand," Hunter protested. "It's a hammer. That's all."

"He's right. We don't know that yet," Bailey said while watching the Corporal bagging the hammer. The Lieutenant continued, "I'll check, but there was a certain entrance wound pattern not from a hammer. Did you find anything else with blood on it?"

"No, that's all," Grand answered.

"Corporal Harlan, go check the car. "

"Hunter, which car is it?"

He said, "Mine. The Blue BMW. But I didn't do anything."

"Is that your hammer on the coffee table?" Bailey asked Hunter.

Hunter looked him directly in his eyes, "I don't usually borrow bloody hammers."

Bailey said, "If we find blood from the victim on the hammer and your fingerprints on it, we'll be taking you downtown."

Grand spoke up, "Officer, we are Quakers. Our family came over here with William Penn, hundreds of years ago. We have never been involved with any type of crime; it is just not in our make-up. This is Marcin Township. Nothing bad ever happens here. It must be someone from outside of the area."

Hunter spoke up, "This is a set-up, I'm telling you. I used the hammer last week to hang a picture. Banged the heck out of my index finger." He held up a bruised finger.

"But why was it found in the car? Do you hang pictures there?" Corporal Harlan asked.

"No, I'm one of those who fears going off the road into a body of water and can't open the door. I do not want to die in my car underwater. With the hammer I can smash the window and escape."

Bailey thought about his own mother, who has the same fear. She has a special tool to smash out the window.

"Was the car window down?" Bailey asked Grand.

"Not the passenger side. I don't know about the other doors."

Bailey asked another question of Hunter. "So, someone, somehow got your car door open, put this hammer in your car, just to get you involved. Oh wait, didn't you see it when you went for donuts?"

"No."

"Grand, where did you find it in the car?" Hunter asked.

She spoke up, "On the passenger side foot carpet."

"So, it was there for all to, see?" Bailey asked.

"We don't know. You're the cops," Hunter said in desperation. "Grand was the only one around my car. You act like I left the bloody hammer there so people would find it. If I killed someone, I sure wouldn't leave evidence in my car in plain view."

"Hunter, I think we need to take a trip downtown," Bailey said in a monotone voice.

Corporal Harlan showed up just then, walking through the front door with more evidence in his hand but wrapped in a bag. He showed it to Bailey. "Found it by the BMW."

"What is it?" Mr. Marcin asked.

Harlan explained, "A cup of half-filled coffee with what looks like blood floating in it and something reddish smeared on the rim."

"That doesn't even make sense," Hunter told them.

"Let's go. We'll hash this out downtown." Lieutenant Bailey led Hunter away, leaving the family reeling from what just happened and anxious to regain normalcy in their lives. At least as much as possible.

Upstairs, Sissy slipped into Joey's room and sat crossed legged on the floor. She watched him playing with his new board game.

A moment later she asked, "Well, Joey?"

"What?"

"Who should be next?"

"I don't know." He was only half listening to her. Too focused on his game.

Sissy continued, "How about we pick a board game, and the winner gets to pick the next person?"

"Okay, but I get to pick the game." Joey said.

"You play them much more than I do." Sissy crossed her arms over her chest and pouted.

Joey said something that shocked her. "Let's pick from the officers downstairs." Then he smiled.

Sissy said excitedly, "Sure, oh, don't forget to put the tin and lead toy horses into the bottom of your toy box, and cover them with the clothes we took from Dad's closet. Some of the shirts have lots of blood on them. If found, the parents will be blamed, not us."

"I already did."

"Good and did you make sure the horse's flowing tail was wiped cleaned of the blood?"

"Done." He replied with his eyes never leaving the board game.

Friends and neighbors always said that the Marcins were blessed with having such wonderful children.

Nancy Bialy Daversa has degrees in English, Behavioral Science, Sociology and Paralegal Studies. She has worked as a Criminal Clerk, even doing night court. Later she became an Executive Television Producer. She has taught at Widener and Immaculata Universities and Rosemount College. She loves investigating whitewashed American history.

ALL DEATHS ENDURE

MATTY DALRYMPLE

"So dear I love him that with him, all deaths I could endure.
Without him, live no life."

John Milton, *Paradise Lost*

At a few minutes before six thirty, the chime of the doorbell echoed down the main hall to the dining room. Andrews made a fine adjustment to the silverware at one of the three place settings, tugged down the vest of his black suit, and walked briskly to the foyer. He opened the door to a thirtyish woman with blond hair, a wisp of which had come loose from the clip which held it back from her pale face. A few flakes of mid-February snow drifted down in the darkness behind her.

"Good evening, miss," he said, stepping aside. "Please come in."

"Thank you." She stepped into the foyer looking, as she had at the time of her last visit a year ago, a bit reluctant.

"May I take your coat?" he asked.

"Thanks." She unbuttoned the coat and turned to let him ease it from her shoulders.

She was wearing a dark blue silk dress with a silver necklace and earrings. He recalled that she had worn the same dress the previous year. It was well made but, he noted, now slightly large for her slender figure.

He hung her coat in a small closet separated from the rest of the foyer by an antique Chinese screen. He emerged and gave a slight bow. "Mrs. Phipps invites you to wait in the library until dinner."

She nodded, rubbing her arms. Andrews had to admit that the foyer wasn't particularly warm. The cost to heat the entire house was prohibitive.

He led her down the central hallway that joined the two-story foyer at the front of the house with the conservatory in back. He turned into a doorway halfway down the hall, then stepped aside to let her enter. A fire crackling in the fireplace held the chill of the foyer and hallway at bay. He had laid the fire himself just before setting the table for dinner.

"Macallan on the rocks?" he asked.

"Yes, thank you."

"One rock," he amended.

She smiled and nodded.

"Dinner at seven, I'll take you to the dining room at six fifty-five," he said, just as a clock on the mantle began to chime half past the hour.

"All right."

He closed the door behind him as he left the library. He had already retrieved the Macallan from the liquor cabinet. He put one ice cube—pleasingly clear since he had boiled the water—in a heavy crystal tumbler, then added two shots of Scotch. He placed the glass on a small silver tray and headed back to the library.

She was standing in front of the fireplace, her arms crossed, gazing into the flames. She started slightly when he cleared his throat to announce his presence. He placed a cocktail napkin on the table closest to where she stood and put her drink on it. "Please make yourself comfortable until dinner is served."

"Thank you." She was taking the first swallow of her drink as he eased the door shut. He returned to the kitchen to make the final preparations for dinner.

At the appointed time, he returned to the library. She was standing by the fire. The tumbler was empty.

"Please follow me, miss."

She smoothed her dress and followed him into the hall and from there to the dining room.

Candles flickered on the table, casting shadows onto the coffered ceiling. The centerpiece was a small arrangement of tulips, cut short so as not to interfere with the diners' conversation. He had removed the leaves from the long table to make it as small and intimate as possible. It was a logistical feat for one person that was getting more difficult to perform with each passing year. He had set three places: one each at the head and foot of the table and one at the side.

"Please have a seat, miss. Mrs. Phipps will be in shortly."

She sat at the side of the table and folded her hands in her lap.

Andrews took his place in the corner. The ticking of the clock seemed loud in the large room.

Just as the clock struck seven, Andrews heard the accustomed tapping on the parquet floor of the hallway. In a moment, Annalise Phipps appeared in the doorway.

Her white hair was coiffed into a perfect and sedate swirl above her fine-featured face, her pink wool dress, as flattering to her petite figure now as it had been when it had been made for her three decades before, accentuating the pinkness of her cheeks. He had retrieved her pearl necklace from the safe deposit box at the bank that afternoon. The cane she carried was more of an accessory than a crutch.

She nodded to him. "Good evening, Andrews."

"Good evening, ma'am."

She crossed the room to the foot of the table. Andrews followed her and pulled out her chair, then adjusted it to her preferred distance from the table. She shook out the linen napkin. The young woman did the same.

"You may serve dinner now, Andrews," Mrs. Phipps said.

He passed through the short hallway that led from the dining room to the kitchen and opened the oven. Inside were three plates topped with metal covers. He put the plates onto a tray and made his careful way back to the dining room. He placed the tray on the sideboard and transferred the plates to the table one at a time: the first to the empty seat at the head of the table, the second to Mrs. Phipps, the third to the young woman. Then he returned to each plate and removed the cover to reveal pork chops, mashed potatoes, and steamed broccoli.

Mrs. Phipps picked up the heavy silver knife and fork in fingers misshapen by arthritis and sliced off a tiny piece of pork chop. She chewed thoughtfully, then patted her mouth with her napkin. "Excellent as always, Andrews."

"Thank you, ma'am."

"What do you think of it, my dear?" asked Mrs. Phipps.

The young woman scooped up a small portion of mashed potatoes, swallowed, and said, "As you say, excellent as always."

Mrs. Phipps smiled at the empty chair at the opposite end of the table. "I'm so glad you like it, my dear. Do you know what today is?"

"It's Valentine's Day. And our anniversary," said the young woman.

"That's right, it is. Happy anniversary, sweetheart."

"Happy anniversary," said the young woman. "My love," she added.

Mrs. Phipps's smile deepened. She cut off another tiny slice of pork chop, chewed and swallowed, and patted her mouth with her napkin again. "I can't believe it's been a whole year, my dear. I have a great deal of news for you."

"Oh yes?" asked the young woman, a hint of trepidation tingeing her voice. "I'm looking forward to hearing what has been happening."

Mrs. Phipps launched into her report of the last year's activities. There were stories of country club dinners, weddings of friends' grandchildren, and a brief trip to Marco Island in December. The young woman nodded and commented, encouraged and, where appropriate, managed an appreciative laugh. As the dinner progressed, her demeanor changed from tense and guarded to cautiously relieved. By the time Andrews returned to the dining room with dessert—chocolate cake he had purchased that after-noon at Wegman's—she was looking merely tired.

The clock struck eight. Mrs. Phipps applied the napkin to her mouth a final time and set it aside. "Andrews?"

He stepped up to her chair and slid it back from the table. She stood and looked toward the empty chair at the head of the table, her eyes brightening with tears. "I must leave now, my dear. I wish we could talk more, but I must admit I'm quite spent. I'm so happy to have been able to update you on what's been going on. Happy Valentine's Day, and happy anniversary." She raised her hand to her mouth and blew a discreet kiss toward the head of the table.

"I'm so happy to have been able to speak with you too, my love," said the young woman.

Annalise Phipps looked toward the empty chair for a few more seconds, a sad smile on her face, then turned and made her way to the door. Andrews stepped ahead of her to open it.

"Thank you, Andrews," she said. "My compliments to the chef," she added playfully.

"Thank you, ma'am."

When he turned back to the table, the young woman was already standing.

He glanced at her plate. She hadn't touched her dessert or, he noted, much of the entree. "Is there anything I can get for you that would be more to your liking, miss?"

"No, thank you," she said. "It was all very good, I'm just not very hungry."

"Certainly, miss."

He stood aside as she stepped out of the dining room into the hallway and preceded him to the foyer. He helped her on with her coat, then pulled an envelope from his inside jacket pocket.

"Please accept this small token of Mrs. Phipps's appreciation," he said, as he always did.

She took the envelope. "Thank you, Andrews."

He knew she wouldn't cash the check. She never did.

IT HAD BEEN four years earlier that he had handed the young woman a check for the first time. Her hand had shaken slightly as she took it.

She had arrived at six thirty and parked her car under the porte cochère as he had requested. At one time there had been a chauffeur who had dealt with visitors' cars, but he had left many years ago for a job in Atlantic City, and Andrews felt uncomfortable enough driving Mrs. Phipps's car—a twenty-year-old Lincoln Town Car—let alone someone else's. That night it had been not snow but a sleety rain forming the backdrop of the young woman's arrival.

He opened the door as she approached it.

"Good evening, miss. My name is Andrews. Please come in."

She stepped into the foyer. "Andrews?" she asked. "Just Andrews?"

"Yes, miss."

"That's very *Upstairs Downstairs*," she said, her mouth beginning to twitch into a smile.

He drew himself up to his full height. "May I take your coat, miss?" he asked severely.

He was gratified to see that that seemed to tamp down the smile.

He hung the coat behind the screen, then led her to the crackling fire in the library and asked her if she would like a cocktail.

"Scotch?" she asked.

"Certainly, miss. Do you have a preferred brand?"

"Macallan?"

"Of course." His humor improved. He prided himself on the Scotch selection in the liquor cabinet—some bottles of which dated back to when he had first stocked it forty years before—and she had redeemed herself somewhat by her choice.

He ascertained her preference for a single ice cube, went to the butler's pantry where the liquor was stored, then returned to the library with the drink on a tray. He put the drink atop a cocktail napkin on the table nearest to where she was standing.

"Ah, I see you've found the music box, miss."

"Yes, it's lovely," she said. "Does it work?"

"Of course." He reached out and gently moved a lever on

the side of the ornately carved wooden case. A metal disk mounted atop the machine, like a warped and perforated album, began to rotate and in a moment the first notes of the *Blue Danube Waltz* filled the room. "Built in 1898," he said. "All original, never restored."

She laughed lightly, delighted.

They listened until the song finished.

"It's wonderful," she said.

He nodded, pleased. "Your husband explained to you about Mrs. Phipps's preference for this ... engagement?"

"Actually, he's my brother—he's also my business manager. He said that Mrs. Phipps is interested in speaking with her husband."

"Yes. And the—um—logistics of the situation? He explained that as well?"

"He said it would be over dinner. I understand that today is their anniversary."

"Yes. Well." He was unsure exactly what Mrs. Phipps's conversation with the brother had been. Mrs. Phipps had gotten the young woman's name from a friend at the country club and had made the phone call herself. He nodded. "I have a few items to attend to, but I'll be back at five till seven to take you to the dining room." He tipped her a small bow and she raised her glass to him.

He returned to the kitchen to complete the dinner preparations. It had been pork chops that night as well, as he recalled.

At the appointed time, he led her to the dining room and seated her at the side of the table, then took his place in the corner.

"This is a beautiful room," she said.

"It is," he said. He was glad that the low light of the candles hid the stains left on the wallpaper from an apparently unfixable leak and the faded silk of the drapes. At least the silver was brightly shined and the crystal buffed. He thought the table looked especially handsome in the flickering light.

"Have you worked for Mrs. Phipps for a long time?"

"Yes, quite a long time."

She appeared to be about to pose another question, then evidently changed her mind. They sat in silence as one minute and then two ticked by.

At seven o'clock, Mrs. Phipps arrived, gave her permission for dinner to be served, and declared it to be delicious.

"How is your pork chop, my dear?" asked Mrs. Phipps, looking toward the empty seat at the head of the table.

The young woman looked at the seat as well, then at Mrs. Phipps, who was gazing expectantly at the empty chair, then at Andrews. He gave her a discreet but, he hoped, encouraging nod.

"Um ... it's very good," she said uncertainly. "Especially the potatoes."

Mrs. Phipps nibbled a delicate forkful of the mashed potatoes and nodded. "Yes." She turned to Andrews. "Very nicely done, Andrews."

"Thank you, ma'am."

Mrs. Phipps put her fork down, clasped her hands in her lap, and leaned forward.

"I know that we're here to celebrate our anniversary, my dear," she said to the empty chair, "but I'm afraid there's something quite serious I must discuss with you."

A silence strung out, the only sound the harsh tick of the clock. Andrews tried to catch the young woman's eye, but she was glancing around the room. Finally, he cleared his throat. She looked toward him, and he gestured toward the empty chair with his head. She looked from the empty chair to Mrs. Phipps, whose posture hadn't changed but whose expression was beginning to look a bit strained. She looked back at Andrews and pointed to herself and then to the chair: *Should I move over there?*

"There's something that Mrs. Phipps would like to discuss with you," he said in a stage whisper, then nodded encouragingly.

"Okay," she said uncertainly.

He nodded more vigorously.

She cleared her throat. "I'm very interested in hearing what you have to discuss," she said to Mrs. Phipps.

The older woman's brow cleared. "You're so thoughtful to listen to my silly concerns, my dear." She fiddled with her teaspoon. "I'm afraid Roger is being ... somewhat irresponsible."

The young woman shot a confused look at Andrews.

"It's so unfortunate that your son would cause you any concern, ma'am," he said.

Mrs. Phipps glanced at him in surprise then said, somewhat reproachfully, "Perhaps you could refill the water glasses, Andrews."

He flushed. No one had yet drunk from the water glasses. He picked up the carafe from the sideboard and added a minuscule amount of water to each glass.

"Thank you, Andrews," she said, clearly feeling she had made her point about such interruptions.

She returned her attention to the head of the table. "As I was saying, it's Roger. He's being somewhat ... excessive in his spending."

After a moment, the young woman said, "I'm sorry to hear that."

"He means well, of course, but he's spending beyond his allowance."

"Allowance?"

"Of course."

"How old is Roger?"

Andrews shook his head vigorously as Mrs. Phipps laughed nervously. "My dear, what a question to ask."

"I'm sorry, it's just that I've got to believe that your son is … um … well into adulthood, and if he's living beyond his means, I don't think you should—" The young woman jumped as the tip of Mrs. Phipps's cane jabbed the floor.

"No."

"I apologize," the young woman said quickly. "It's not my place—" She winced as the cane cracked down again.

"No!"

There was a fraught silence, the young woman looking between Mrs. Phipps and Andrews. The grandfather clock ticked relentlessly from a dim corner of the room.

Finally, the young woman took a deep breath. "Mrs. Phipps, I don't think—"

"Nooooo!" The exclamation—more a cry than a word— ripped from Annalise Phipps's throat. She stood, drew the cane over her head, and smashed it down onto the table. A crystal goblet shattered, spilling water across the table and shards of glass across the room. The young woman pushed her chair back from the table so quickly that she almost sent herself over backwards. Andrews sprang forward and tried to grab the cane.

"Ma'am, please—"

Mrs. Phipps swiped blindly behind her, catching Andrews in the elbow with the tip of the cane. He jumped back, cradling his arm.

"I'm talking—" She brought the cane down again, this time connecting with the plate, whose two halves left the table on opposite sides.

"—to my—" The next blow rattled the silver and sent a saltshaker rolling toward the edge of the table.

"—husband!" The final blow was a glancing one and caught the vase of tulips. Water and flowers tumbled off the table and landed on the floor at the feet of the young woman.

Mrs. Phipps paused to catch her breath, and Andrews quickly approached and grasped the cane.

"Ma'am, please don't distress yourself."

Mrs. Phipps hitched a breath, looked toward the empty chair at the head of the table, and burst into tears.

"There, there, ma'am," said Andrews, taking the cane and lowering her into her chair. "It's all right."

Mrs. Phipps dropped her face into her hands, sobs racking her body.

The young woman stood, watching with wide eyes.

"I'm sure that Mr. Phipps has something useful to say about Roger." He looked pleadingly at the young woman.

She sank back down onto her chair. The clock marked time. Finally, she spoke.

"It's me, my dear."

"My love," said Andrews, sotto voce.

"My love," amended the young woman.

Mrs. Phipps took a gulp of air and, without raising her eyes, said, "Really?"

"Yes, really," said the young woman, deepening her voice slightly.

Mrs. Phipps looked up at the empty chair at the head of the table.

"You're here?"

"Yes, I'm here. And I'm so glad we have this opportunity to talk about Roger. I don't want you facing such a difficult situation by yourself."

Mrs. Phipps gave a weak smile. "I'm so relieved. And I'm

so sorry to have behaved that way. I don't know what came over me." She blotted her eyes with her napkin.

"Completely understandable, my love."

Mrs. Phipps turned to Andrews. "I'm afraid I may have caught you with the cane, Andrews. I'm terribly sorry. Are you all right?

"Quite all right, ma'am."

"Why don't you tell me what Roger's been up to?" said the young woman.

"Yes, my dear, I'm anxious to get your advice."

And Mrs. Phipps unburdened herself to her husband about the trials and tribulations of dealing with their oldest son: the unwise investments, the profligate spending, an unsuccessful marriage—his third—that would no doubt result in another costly alimony payment.

The young woman at the side of the table sympathized, made helpful—although, as Andrews noted gratefully, not too specific—suggestions, and congratulated Mrs. Phipps on her sensitive handling of the difficult matters.

Eventually the clock struck eight and Mrs. Phipps heaved a relieved sigh and stood. Andrews was at her side in a moment with the cane.

"I can't tell you how much this conversation has meant to me, my dear," she said. "I feel so much better prepared to deal with whatever Roger may get up to next."

"You're doing wonderfully, my love," said the young woman.

Mrs. Phipps took the cane from Andrews and looked down at the mess of smashed food and broken crystal at her place. "Andrews, I'm afraid I've made quite a mess of your lovely dinner, but I'm sure it would have been excellent as always."

"May I bring a snack up to your room, ma'am?"

"Oh no, thank you. I'm fine for this evening."

She turned toward the head of the table. "I miss you so much, my dear."

"And I miss you, too, my love."

"I remember exactly where I was standing on our wedding day when you told me you would always be with me on our anniversary—on Valentine's Day. And even with all the traveling you had to do, you always were."

"Yes."

"Even now."

"Yes, even now."

"Until next year, then?"

The young woman hesitated only briefly. "Yes, my love, until next year."

Mrs. Phipps tapped her way to the door, leaning on her cane hardly at all. She turned at the door, blew a kiss off her twisted fingers toward the head of the table, and disappeared into the hallway, the tap of her cane receding toward the conservatory.

The young woman stood and followed Andrews wordlessly down the hall toward the foyer. He pulled her coat from the closet behind the screen and held it up for her. It took her a few tries to get her arm into the coat sleeve.

As she buttoned the coat, he drew an envelope from his inside jacket pocket. "Please accept this small token of Mrs. Phipps's appreciation."

She buried her hands in the pockets of her coat. "But I didn't do anything. Her husband wasn't there."

"I'm sure Mrs. Phipps would want you to have this for taking the time to come by this evening."

Her hands stayed in her pockets. "People pay me to see the dead, and sometimes to speak with them. It doesn't always work. Sometimes the people aren't there, or sometimes they're there and I can't see them, or can't communicate with them. In any case, I don't charge for ..." She hesitated. "Well, for pretending."

"Please. She's ..." He cleared his throat. "You've been a tremendous help."

She took the envelope reluctantly and stuffed it into her pocket without looking at it.

"Next year at the same time, miss?"

There was a long pause, then finally she said, "Yes. All right."

"Thank you, miss."

She nodded.

He opened the door for her, letting a cold breeze into the foyer.

She stepped outside, her foot finding a puddle that had managed to form even under the protection of the porte cochère. He must see to the hole in the roof, he thought. She climbed into her car, and Andrews stood at the entrance until she had passed through the rusting metal gates and turned onto the Main Line street. Then he stepped into the relative warmth of the foyer and closed and locked the door behind him.

He went to the small room off the kitchen that he used as his office and where he kept the notebook in which he recorded appointments. He flipped forward twelve pages, one month per page, then noted in an unsteady, crabbed hand: *February 14 6:30-8:00 p.m. Ann Kinnear.*

Matty Dalrymple is the author of the Lizzy Ballard Thrillers, beginning with *Rock Paper Scissors*; the Ann Kinnear Suspense Novels, beginning with *The Sense of Death*; and the Ann Kinnear Suspense Shorts, including *Close These Eyes*. She is a member of

International Thriller Writers and Sisters in Crime. Matty also podcasts, writes, speaks, and consults on the writing craft and the publishing voyage as The Indy Author. She has written books on the business of short fiction and podcasting for authors, and her articles have appeared in *Writer's Digest* magazine. She is a member of the Alliance of Independent Authors.

WHERE ARE THE DOGS?

DIANE KIDDY

*Y*ou move through life, oblivious to what lies ahead. The choices you make when you're young seem okay. Then decades later you find yourself without the relationships you assumed would be there.

Whether you make the right decisions or not, "It's a crap-shoot," as my friend Elizabeth used to say. Those around you, through their actions, may adversely affect what you want and strive toward. Maybe it is a matter of fate or the positioning of celestial objects in the solar system. Some believe in the hands of God or another power that controls the universe.

When you were working, you didn't get to spend much time at home. The picturesque enclave of Tudor style houses overlooking the Schuylkill River where you live is called East Falls. Within walking distance is the Wissahickon section of Fairmount Park as well as Main Street in Manayunk. It's a great location. The commute to downtown Philadelphia only takes about twelve minutes depending on traffic. You envision the route along Kelly Drive, past Boathouse Row, around the Art Museum circle, on to the Benjamin Franklin

Parkway adorned with the colorful flags of different nations, and finally to City Hall. Your designated parking space was at the northeast corner of that grand structure.

You miss your profession and local politics, and the self-image you built based on a distinguished career. But at least yours is not "a life of quiet desperation," as William oft quotes Thoreau in describing his own tribulations.

You followed your passion in medicine to lead Philadelphia's Department of Health for almost nine years. This period included the beginning of the pandemic through the first phase of vaccinations. As is customary, you stayed on until the incoming mayor appointed his own Health Commissioner. It's still a shock to no longer experience the adrenaline flow of being on-call 24/7 to deal with COVID and manage the unknown. Your team of physicians, RNs and other public health professionals made a difference, enabling the city government to respond rapidly to multiple surges of infection. You saved lives, and now you must save your own.

Lately, you've become suspicious about the lack of activity at the house situated directly behind yours. It is the third morning in a row that the coonhounds are not charging around and trying to ascend your fence. They consistently create a ruckus during their first run of the day. This Wednesday, it is quiet, without their athletic antics.

The black and brown dogs - Nick, Amar, and Clara - are siblings who used to live on your side of the ivy-covered chain-link border. When your ex-husband William returned to Philadelphia after six years in the Caribbean, he reclaimed the pack of dogs left in your care during his absence. Now your daily routine is to watch them play from the vantage point of your bedroom window. Upon the seventh peal of the bells of St. Bridget's, you always arise to enjoy this simple pleasure.

Putting aside some initial doubts, you endorsed William's

plan of renting the adjacent property since it was available. Although you divorced a long time ago, a bond exists which has never been broken. It is a matter of respecting each other's privacy while being supportive as needed or desired. This ongoing attachment interfered with progress on the dating front through the years – that and your allegiance to keeping brutal hours at the office.

William hadn't mentioned going out of town. And if he were away on a trip, why bring the dogs? So where is everybody? Against your better judgement, you walk around to the side of his house, where there's a gate with a latch. You noiselessly enter the garden, admiring the pink and white azalea bushes in full bloom. As you peer in the windows along the back of the medium-sized, brick building, your anxiety increases. There is no evidence so far of living creatures on the ground floor. You inspect the detached garage and see that a red and white Mini Cooper is parked inside. Odd. William doesn't own a car. He lost his driver's license years ago due to a DUI and never reapplied. He declares it's safer for him to be off the road. Whenever he was going to the airport or train station, he'd take an Uber or ask you for a ride.

But wait a minute. William had decided to leave the islands as soon as it was safe to travel, to hunker down in more familiar surroundings during the pandemic. So, why take a chance and go anywhere now?

In Philadelphia, masking is still required indoors. Most citizens remain cautious given the waves of Omicron and its variants. However, many people insist that soon things will be normal again. Frankly, you do not hold that optimistic opinion. Nor do you agree that the past norm is worth recovering. In short, you're prepared to wear a mask, eat outside, and keep your distance from others – except for the dogs, and William, of course.

Where is everybody?

Upon finishing your inspection and returning home, you find something stuffed through the mail slot in your front door. As you enter the hall, a sheet of paper flutters to the floor. The door is still ajar as you stoop to examine a notice addressed to you. Then you head to the kitchen where you pour a cup of Darjeeling tea. As you sip the hot beverage, the phone on the wall rings. Usually, you don't pay attention to the landline, but on an impulse, you grab the receiver. The connection is crackly, and you can barely decipher the words of a female voice. However, there is no mistaking the background noise of a dog. It's a bark you know well. Whoever this woman is, she must have Nick with her. First, you feel relief, followed by concern.

Her message is the same as the printed one you read just a few minutes ago. William, and the dogs too, must be in imminent danger. Gasping, breathless, you spin around at the sound of the front door slamming shut. Unfathomably, there is the sound of a key turning in the lock. You race to the screened porch, and then back to the kitchen, discovering that all doors to the house are locked from the outside. The warnings are too late. You are a prisoner in your own home, although not due to COVID like so many others. And William and the dogs are gone.

You tiptoe back to the front door and peer through the small leaded glass window at the top. No one is visible on the steps. You gingerly apply pressure to the knob and the door easily flings open. With renewed confidence, you circle William's house again searching for the dogs. Amar is lying next to Clara, and both are sleeping. Nick is stretching after his mid-morning nap. The sun shines bright from high in the sky. The church bells chime ten times. You hear approaching footsteps from the house next door. William? No. An unfamiliar man in his mid-thirties with a broad smile on his face comes into view. Who is this person? Why is he trespassing on William's property?

"Hello, Dr. McCotter. How are you today?"

You study him as he joins you by the gate, but do not have any idea about his identity. Wait, is he the one who took the dogs? Did he lock the doors of your house? You begin to back away from him. Does he have something to do with William's disappearance as well?

Before completing that last thought, a brown-skinned woman suddenly appears from the other direction. She calls out your name. Is she the one who telephoned earlier? You aren't sure, but her lilting voice sounds familiar.

"Dr. McCotter, it's time to come inside for breakfast, or should I say brunch at this hour. Although I notice you already had some caffeine to start the day."

You focus your attention on the young woman as she continues to explain something to you. She is wearing what resembles a uniform, like those blue scrubs worn in hospitals. A badge is clipped to the fabric at the neck of her shirt. You strain your eyes to read it. Does it say Shirley, or Sheila? It is difficult to make out as her braids partially cover the name. However, the Penn emblem you recognize, as the University of Pennsylvania is your alma mater.

"Like I told you, Doc, I have such bad luck. The 48 bus was late, so I had to take the 32 and walk the rest of the way. But here I am!" she exclaims.

You scrutinize the woman's face before shifting your gaze to the strange man who continues to grin. You recheck the other yard for any signs of dogs asleep or awake. There are none. Shirley, or Sheila, moves behind you to gently take your arm, guiding you toward your house. She is chattering about the transportation problem and some other nonsense. Without resistance, you amble alongside her. At the entryway, she picks up a colorful flyer, with a picture of a hound, describing a grooming business.

"Are you reconsidering getting another one?" she asks and hands you the advertisement.

What on earth is she talking about now? Slowly it dawns on you that she must be referring to a dog. You ignore the question, inhale deeply, and uncertainly inquire as to the whereabouts of William.

Shirley, or Sheila, leads you into the living room to the leather sofa by the fireplace. You sink slowly into the cushions, watching closely the woman's movements. She takes the picture frame from the end table and puts it in your lap. You do not lower your eyes as you already know it is an old photograph of William. Recently, you've been looking longingly at it every morning and evening. You also know that William is not in Philadelphia. Sadly, he did not return from Jamaica in time to beat COVID. You'll never forget that telephone conversation with the nurse at the hospital in Port Antonio, confirmed by an official letter about William's unexpected passing. Afterwards, you secluded yourself inside for weeks with the doors and windows closed, sitting in the same place staring at nothing. That's when your nephew suggested that you engage an assistant, as he termed it. Regarding the coonhounds, each of those dear dogs lived a long life and died peacefully at home with you. Nick was the last one to go only a couple of months ago. Oh, how you miss the constant canine comfort which eased the emptiness. But to answer the aide's question, you are not ready to welcome a new furry fellow into your heart and home.

Your memories imprison you, sometimes making it hard to distinguish reality from the musings of a muddled mind. Your periods of lucidity are not necessarily preferable to your deliberate deflection from the daily devastation you experience. What you don't want to remember is that you're alone. The canine contact you counted on is no longer present. The human happiness you crave cannot be obtained. You try to forget that the killer, COVID, tragically took your true love just before being reunited. So, you regularly reimagine any other scenario to explain why they are all gone. Your consciousness constructs a different existence. And then you inevitably force yourself to face the terrible truth.

DIANE KIDDY, a member of Sisters in Crime for 30 years, contributed to three prior Delaware Valley chapter anthologies and has also written under the name D.K. Lillian. Born in Philadelphia, Diane resides in the East Falls section of the city with her beagle Mae. She is active politically and her career spans the public and private sectors in health and human services administration.

BLOOD OF THE WICKED

MATTY DALRYMPLE AND JANE GORMAN

The righteous shall rejoice when he seeth the vengeance: He shall wash his feet in the blood of the wicked.

Psalms 58:10

Adam Kaminski scanned the entrance hall of Germantown's Whistler-Talbot House. Its appearance tonight would surprise the history buffs who were its most frequent visitors. In previous years, they might have expected the entrance hall of the colonial-era building to be decorated for Thanksgiving: pumpkins flanking fireplaces, cornucopias spilling yellow and orange gourds, harvest wheat, and cinnamon sticks. A few months ago, they would have encountered an interior stripped of most of its furnishings, since these had been covered or removed to protect them during an extensive renovation of the historic home. Without the antique rugs covering the worn wood floors and portraits of famous residents hiding the cracked walls, the house showed its age—and not in a good way.

And all that was before Adam's Philadelphia Police Department colleagues had affixed police tape to the entrances and erected high wattage lights to illuminate the crime scene.

Adam snapped on one of the lights that was mounted on a stand in a corner of the entrance hall.

Ann Kinnear, one of the two other visitors accompanying Adam on this night's visit, raised a hand to shield her eyes. "Do we really need that? It's going to make it hard for me to do my job." He put her in her early thirties—about his own age—with reddish-blond hair caught back in a ponytail. She was dressed for the chilly November night in an outfit that appeared to be sourced entirely from L.L. Bean.

Adam let out a slow breath, focusing on keeping his cool and not letting his skepticism show. "Sorry. I should have guessed you'd need it to be dark." He switched off the light and turned on the hallway's chandelier. The two working electric "candles" cast a dim glow across the space.

Through the open front door, Adam could see Germantown Avenue. If it hadn't been for the cars parked at meters and the electrical lines running over the trolley track embedded in the concrete median of the cobblestone street, he suspected that this stretch of the avenue didn't look much different now than it had when the brick and stone buildings lining it had been built in the eighteenth century.

Tonight, pockets of mist hung below the streetlamps, and the third member of the party, lingering by the door, had carried the weather in with him. Gray hair, frizzled clumps in the moist air, stuck out below his National Park Service ranger hat. He pulled a tissue out of a pocket and swiped it across his nose.

The poor guy had no idea why Adam had requested

admittance to the building at this time of night. Adam hadn't wanted to alarm him—or embarrass himself.

"Thanks for letting us in, Thurman," Adam said. "Do you need me to call you when we're done, or can we lock up ourselves?"

"Oh, I can lock up when we're done," said Thurman, closing and locking the door behind him.

"You're staying?"

"Yes. It's the rules—no unescorted visitors in Park Service sites."

Adam suppressed a groan. So much for avoiding having a witness for the evening's event. He liked the old ranger, who served as a docent at the site and had volunteered to be the Philly PD's Park Service liaison. More than once, Adam had come upon Thurman regaling a surprised patrol officer with tales of the home's historic past or sharing details of the Battle of Germantown with a crime scene tech. In fact, on the night of the murder, Thurman had been at the nearby Germantown Friends School, trying to inspire a group of students with stories about their hometown's past.

Unfortunately, Thurman was almost the only person connected with the house and the case whom the police could place at the time of the murder. Adam had spent hours poring through alibis from the victim's family, co-workers, acquaintances, park staff, and contractors, looking for a fact —or gap—that might expose the killer. He had followed up every lead he could, given he was stuck working this one on his own. Between a series of jewelry store robberies, a shooting in Old Town, and a drowning in the Schuylkill that may or may not have been murder, the department was stretched thin. If he had come up with something, anything, he wouldn't have been taking Ann Kinnear on this house tour.

"Tell Ann what you told me," he said to Thurman.

"Sure thing." Thurman squeezed past Adam and Ann and made his way down the hall to where the stairway rose to the second floor. "I noticed the blood on the stairs first, then I saw a couple of drops leading toward the back door."

Ann peered at the stairs and the rough boards of the hallway floor. "I don't see anything."

Adam crossed his arms, and a smile flitted across his lips. "Maybe if the light was a little brighter—"

She shot him a look. "No. The light is fine."

"Actually," said Thurman, "once the police got the samples they needed, they gave us the okay to clean things up." He dabbed at his nose again. "At first, I thought maybe one of the workers had gotten hurt. I looked out back, but the blood drops petered out. So I came back inside and went up the stairs. There was more blood the further up I went. It led to the back bedroom." He shuddered. "I don't like to think about it."

"He found the body," Adam explained to Ann. He turned back to the ranger. "Thurman, you can stay down here if you want. I can take Ann upstairs."

"No," said Thurman, rallying. "Rules are rules." He tucked his tissue in his pocket, took a deep breath, and led them up the stairs. When they reached the second floor, he gestured down the hall, toward the back of the house. "I found him in the back bedroom." He swallowed audibly and turned his hat nervously in his hands. "Actually, if it's okay with the two of you, I think I'll wait here."

"Sure," said Adam. "We'll let you know if we have any questions."

Thurman stepped back to let them pass, and Adam led Ann down the hall to the last door and stepped into the room.

Because the renovation activities hadn't reached this room, the furnishings—a small wooden chair and a bulky canopy bed—were still in place. A window that would have given a view over the back yard and neighboring houses was covered by a heavy wooden shutter, closed now as it had been when Adam first arrived on the crime scene.

Ann glanced around the room. "You said the victim was heading up the construction project?"

"That's right. Bill Brackney."

"It doesn't look like any work was being done here. Why was he even in this room?"

"Good question." He arched an eyebrow. "I guess there's some idea that you might be able to answer it. That's why you're here, right? To answer the unanswerable questions?" The absurdity of the situation struck him, and he suppressed a smile. He needed at least to appear to be taking this seriously.

Ann didn't bother to return his look. "I don't know the answers myself, I just talk to the people who do."

He sighed. "We don't know why Brackney would have come up here. As far as we know, at that time of night, he had no reason to venture out of the kitchen, which he was using as an office. According to the crew, he did paperwork there in the evenings, after the rest of them left."

"I read in the news that the murder weapon was an antique poker."

"That's what we think." Adam gestured to a small fire-place with a decorative tile surround. "Thurman confirmed that a poker that's usually in the room is missing. Based on the injuries, the coroner thinks that it could have been the murder weapon."

"And you haven't found it."

"No."

"The fact that the killer used a weapon he found in the house could mean that it wasn't premeditated, right?"

Her back was to him, and Adam rolled his eyes. This was

a complete waste of time, as he'd known it would be. She was just going over the same ground he'd already covered. "Now you're investigating? I thought you were here to report information you got from your," he cleared his throat, "sources."

She turned to face him and crossed her arms. "Detective, I don't have to be here. In fact, I don't particularly *want* to be here. I'm not even being paid for this engagement—I'm doing it as a favor for Detective Booth. You give the word and I'm out of here."

Adam thought back to the call he had gotten from fellow Philly detective Joe Booth—practical, unflappable Booth—suggesting that Adam bring in someone named Ann Kinnear to check out the crime scene.

"I doubt she's going to find anything that our guys missed," Adam said to Joe as he sorted through his mental files for why the name sounded familiar.

"You might be surprised," Joe replied, a smile in his voice, before filling Adam in on Ann's special skill.

It only was after they ended the call, Adam even then regretting that he couldn't easily withdraw his acceptance of Joe's suggestion, when the name finally clicked into place.

"Oh, God," he groaned. "Not *that* Ann Kinnear."

His cousin Dan's former flame.

He had called Dan, expecting to share a couple of gently mocking stories about Dan's crazy ex-girlfriend. However, much to Adam's surprise, Dan—who would never knock on wood or throw salt over his shoulder—joined Joe in vouching for Ann's ability. Adam could even recall a Kaminski family get-together many years earlier when Dan had made fun of Adam and a couple of other cousins for playing with a Ouija board.

Adam trusted Dan. He trusted Joe Booth. The idea might seem crazy, but at this point, he had exhausted his less crazy options.

Adam raised a conciliatory hand to Ann. "Look, I'm sorry. I didn't realize you'd care about the details of the investigation. Don't you just …" He waved his hand to take in the entire house. "… walk around? I guess I don't know how this is supposed to work."

Ann dropped her arms to her sides. "The more I know, the more effectively I can *just walk around.*" She scanned the room. "The killer was definitely a man?"

"Or an incredibly strong woman, I suppose," said Adam, "considering the injuries Brackney sustained."

"Did someone break in?"

"No. There's no evidence of a break-in, and everyone says that Brackney was diligent about locking the house when he was working here alone."

"So how did his killer get in?"

Adam hesitated, weighing how much of his speculation about the crime he should share. Then he decided there was no harm. After all, who would believe anything this woman reported about her visit? "It could have been someone he knew and trusted. The killer might have had access to a key or been hiding in the house when Brackney locked up."

"Did the other people working on the project have keys?"

"No. There was only one key for the whole crew, and Brackney usually had it. On days he wasn't working, he'd pass it to whoever the supervisor was going to be that day."

"So, what's the popular theory?"

"My boss is leaning toward it being gang related. In fact, the victim normally wore a heavy gold chain, and it wasn't found on his body, so the theory is that he crossed the wrong people, and someone killed him to send a message. Or he owed them money, and they took the chain as partial payment. But I know the gangs that cover this territory. This killing … let's just say it wasn't their style. Not even close."

"What does that mean?"

"They have their own trademarks. When they kill some-one, they want everyone to know they were responsible. They administer a certain type of beating, they take a certain type of trophy. But we didn't find any of those markers here."

"You said that his chain was missing. Maybe that was the trophy."

"That's not the kind of trophy they take."

She grimaced. "Ah. Gotcha." After a pause, she continued. "Maybe it was just someone who meant to steal the chain and things got out of control."

"I checked all the local pawnshops. It hasn't shown up anywhere."

"So Bill Brackney had no enemies—?"

"I didn't say that. Word was he was cheating on his wife, and she recently filed for divorce after he slapped her during an argument at a Phillies game."

Ann raised her eyebrows. "Seems like a viable motive."

"She has an airtight alibi—video from a bar she was at."

"It seems like a historic building like this would have security video ..."

"The cameras are on a circuit that had been turned off because of the construction."

"Someone associated with the project would have known that. Maybe the killer was an unhappy employee."

Adam stuffed his hands in his pockets. "There's a carpenter he fired about a month ago, guy called Rinaldi, but it's not like the guy had any trouble finding other work. You can imagine he might have been pissed—but killing mad? You'd have to be a pretty damn unhappy employee to do what the killer did to Brackney." He ran his fingers through his hair. "And why would Brackney let a former worker— one he'd fired—into the house after hours? It makes no sense. No one's buying the carpenter as a serious suspect." He laughed softly. "Plus, he's an Eagle Scout. Seriously, an actual

Eagle Scout. He'd have any judge eating out of his hand." He shrugged. "In any case, he's lawyered up and we don't have any real evidence against him."

"So, dead end … so to speak?"

Adam suppressed a shiver. It felt colder in the room than it had outside. "I don't know. There was something about the carpenter … I'm willing to believe he's involved in some way, but I'm not sure how. There's nothing to tie him to the house that night—in fact, no evidence that he ever came here or even saw Brackney after he was fired." He heaved a sigh. "So, have you got anything for me?"

"Not yet," said Ann, "but we should check the rest of the house."

ANN KINNEAR FOLLOWED Thurman up the stairs to the third floor of the house, Adam Kaminski bringing up the rear. As the ranger teetered up the steps, Ann wondered if the Park Service had any physical requirements for rangers. She'd hate to think of Thurman charged with leading history buffs through Valley Forge at the height of summer or scrambling up the waterfront cliffs in Acadia. On the other hand, maybe that was why he was assigned to this site, where the biggest threat might not be sunstroke or a heart attack but making it from the historic site to one's car after dark.

She peered into each room, mostly tuning out the elderly ranger's running commentary and trying not to be disconcerted by how much Adam Kaminski resembled his cousin Dan. He even had Dan's dimples.

When they completed the tour—no joy upstairs—and returned to the entrance hall, she wondered idly how awkward it would be if she continued through the front door, out to her Forester, and home to Kennett Square. She wasn't happy about going to the trouble to accommodate Joe Booth's request, only to be insulted by a cop with a chip on his shoulder.

Before Ann got the call from Joe asking her to help out a fellow detective, she had assumed any unofficial work she did for the Philadelphia Police Department would be for him. When she got an email from her former boyfriend Dan asking her to take the job, she was even more surprised. Although Ann and Dan had since reconciled, their breakup had been precipitated by Dan's disbelief in her ability. It wasn't until years later, when Ann ran into Dan and his wife, Amita, and spoke to their little girl, Sylvia, that Dan believed.

Sylvia had died a year earlier.

When Ann, Thurman, and Adam reached the first-floor entrance hall, the ranger herded them toward the back of the house. "More to see on this floor."

They wandered through a few rooms, some bare of furnishings, some with a sheet-draped stack in the middle.

"Anything?" asked Adam. He smiled, but Ann could tell it was forced.

"I'd let you know if there was."

She never liked to disappoint a client, even a non-paying one, but a failure on this assignment would be especially galling. It was clear that Adam thought she was a charlatan. She would love to prove him wrong.

When they reached the end of the hallway, Thurman pulled open a wooden door with a heavy cast-iron handle and bolt. "Last room—the kitchen." He flicked a switch next to the door, but the room remained dark, lit only by the light leaking in from the hallway and the large, unshuttered window overlooking the back yard. "These lights must be on one of the circuits that are turned off for the construction. Want a flashlight?"

"No," said Ann, "this is fine."

As her eyes adjusted, she saw that this room was more fully furnished than the other rooms on the first floor. Over-size utensils hung over a fireplace big enough for a man to walk into. Rough wooden benches flanked a heavy wooden table, its surface scarred by the blades of countless knives and cleavers. Someone—Thurman?—had even arranged fake fruits and meats on pewter trays on the table to make the room look lived in.

However, as far as she could tell, the room was uninhabited.

Damn.

She was weighing the pros and cons of offering to make a return visit on another night when she noticed a doorway on the other side of the room. It would have been invisible in the near darkness if not for a faint light emanating from the adjoining space.

"What's that?" she asked, pointing.

"The scullery," replied Thurman. "Hardly more than a closet."

Ann crossed to the doorway and looked into the room.

"Flashlight?" Thurman asked again.

"No need," said Ann, not bothering to keep the satisfaction out of her voice. "I can see what I need to see."

A young woman—Ann guessed she was in her late teens—stood at the back of the small space, arms folded, her expression a combination of adult defiance and childlike sullenness. Her clothing suggested that she had been an early inhabitant of the house: an ankle-length linen dress covered by a patched apron, low-heeled shoes, and a cap of ruffled white cotton. The only spot of color was the blue ribbon that trimmed the cap.

The girl's eyes widened when Ann met her gaze. As a spirit, she was obviously unaccustomed to being seen. In fact, Ann suspected that if she had been a servant, as her clothing and her location in the scullery suggested, she might have been unaccustomed to being "seen" even when she was alive.

"Hello," said Ann.

"What is it?" asked Adam.

Ann turned back to where Adam stood near the door to the hallway. "There's someone here."

"You found the ghost of Bill Brackney in the scullery?" asked Adam, deadpan. "That's a surprise."

"It's not Brackney. It's a young woman. From a very long time ago, I'm guessing." She turned back to the girl. "I'm Ann. What's your name?"

After a moment, the girl answered, somewhat reluctantly. "Priscilla."

"Pleased to meet you, Priscilla."

Priscilla dropped her arms and fiddled with a bit of rough lace on one sleeve. "How come you can see me?"

"It's an ability I've had for as long as I remember. It's my business now—people hire me to talk with the dead."

Priscilla examined her speculatively for a moment, then asked, "How about the other two? Do they talk to dead people, too?"

"No, but I can help you talk with them if you'd like."

Priscilla took a tentative step toward the door and peeked out into the kitchen. Then she stepped back, her expression less sullen. "I've seen them before. Who's the tall one?"

"His name is Adam. The other one is Thurman."

Priscilla patted a stray wisp of hair into place. "Can Adam see me?"

"No. At least I don't think so."

Priscilla's expression fell. "That's too bad."

Ann suppressed a smile. It looked like Detective Kaminski had a young admirer. "Do you want to come out and meet them?"

"I don't need to meet the little one," said Priscilla. "I know all I need to know about him."

Ann turned to the ranger. "Thurman, I think Priscilla would be more comfortable with less of a crowd. If you wouldn't mind …?"

Thurman, who was already backing toward the door to the hallway, nodded vigorously. "Sure, sure. I'll be right outside if you need anything." He stepped through the doorway and pulled the door shut behind him.

The girl relaxed visibly. She stepped out of the scullery and shot a coy look at Adam.

"Priscilla," said Ann, "may I introduce Adam."

"Hello, Priscilla," said Adam, natural politeness evidently trumping disbelief.

Priscilla blushed and bobbed a little curtsy. "Is he your husband?" she asked Ann.

"No, he's a police detective. He's investigating a murder that took place in the house."

Priscilla stiffened.

"Did you know that someone had been murdered?" Ann asked.

After a moment, Priscilla nodded. Her eyes drifted to Adam and back to Ann. The pause was longer this time, then she asked, "Is the short one a police detective?"

"No, Thurman is a National Park Service ranger."

"National Park Service ranger?" repeated Priscilla, enunciating the unfamiliar phrase carefully. "He's responsible for protecting the house."

Priscilla shifted her gaze to Adam. "The tall one looks more like a protector. Maybe once he catches the killer, he'll be grateful for your help and ask you to marry him."

Ann's laugh elicited a look of surprise from Priscilla and raised eyebrows from Adam.

"I'm pretty sure that won't happen," said Ann, tamping

down her amusement, "but I know he would be very grateful to you."

Priscilla smiled wistfully. "Too bad he can't ask *me* to marry him."

Ann wasn't prepared to endure too much more of Priscilla mooning over Adam. "So, the murder ... did you see it happen?"

Priscilla's expression sobered and she gave one quick nod of her head.

"Will you tell me what happened?" Ann asked.

Priscilla was silent for so long that Ann thought she was going to refuse, but finally she heaved a sigh and said, "Yes. If it will help Adam. And of course you too, Ann," she added graciously.

Ann smiled. "Thank you, Priscilla." She gestured toward the table. "Can you sit down with us?"

Priscilla nodded and followed Ann to the table. She sat on one side, Ann and Adam on the other. "I saw it happen ..." she began.

Priscilla stood by the window in the front room, looking out at the nighttime scene. She had never gotten used to how the lights suspended over the street made it almost as easy to see at night as during the day. She had never lingered in this room when she was alive, only hurried in and out to lay the fire or collect the ashes. She enjoyed taking advantage of the view now that she had the run of the house.

It also kept her out of the way of Bill, who was at his usual place in the kitchen.

The people who came to the house these days no longer used the kitchen to prepare food, but as a sort of study. She gathered that Bill was in charge of the workers who arrived carrying hammers and drills and other tools Priscilla didn't recognize. He often worked late into the evening, shuffling through papers, or tapping on the lettered keys on the book-sized machine he put on the table or on the tiny machine he held in his hand.

With a sigh, she turned away from the window, crossed the room, and wandered down the hallway and up the stairs to the top floor. This window gave a view through the branches of the locust trees that grew behind the house, a few of which had been saplings when she was alive, and into the surrounding lots. The view was better now that the leaves had fallen, but less interesting since there were fewer people out as the weather got colder.

Tonight, though, she saw a figure, almost indistinguishable in the darkness, moving through the back yard. Was it one of the young women whom Bill 'entertained'—her mouth twisted in distaste—in the kitchen? She had retired here to the top floor on more than one occasion when Bill and his visitor put the kitchen to a use better suited to a bedchamber. For a time, the visitor had been a pretty, dark-haired girl about the same age as Priscilla. He called her Evie. Then it was an even younger girl he called Abby. Then a redhead he called Ginger. None of them wore wedding rings. Even if they had, they obviously weren't married to Bill who, until recently, had worn a wedding ring that he took off before his visitors arrived. Now the only jewelry he wore was a heavy gold necklace. She'd never get used to the idea of a working man wearing a necklace.

She was surprised when she didn't hear the door thump closed behind the new arrival, but instead saw the figure moving away. Then she saw another figure moving toward the house. The second, bigger figure passed the first on its way to the back door. She heard footsteps on the stairs leading from the yard to the back door and the faint squeak of the door opening, a rectangle of lights spilling out across the back yard. Which of the girls would it be tonight?

Although, she realized, perhaps it wasn't one of Bill's girls. She had heard him mention to the workers the importance of keeping the building locked, especially after dark. Bill himself was always diligent about locking the door, and when he heard a knock, he always peered out through the spy hole before he opened it to the visitor.

But she hadn't heard a knock. Did one of the figures moving through the back yard tonight have a key?

The smaller figure remaining in the yard turned back toward the house for a moment, illuminated briefly in the light from the open door, then turned again and hurried away.

The visitors were not Bill's girls. They were not girls at all.

Priscilla heard voices from the first floor.

She turned from the window and hurried down the stairs.

ADAM TRIED to keep his gaze on Ann as she relayed what she was supposedly hearing from the dead Priscilla. However, her rendition of a person actually conveying information provided by another party was so convincing that he couldn't help periodically glancing toward where the spirit supposedly sat across from him.

"Priscilla, did you recognize the person you saw in the light from the doorway?" Ann asked.

Priscilla must have responded in the affirmative.

"Can you tell me who it was?"

Another pause, then Ann looked at the door leading from the kitchen to the hallway, eyebrows raised. "Thurman?"

"Thurman?" echoed Adam.

He heard the squeak of metal and a thump—the cast iron latch falling into place—then the pounding of running feet retreating down the hallway.

Adam jumped for the door and tried to push it open, but it stayed firmly closed. "Damn!"

He stepped back and slammed his foot onto the wood over the latch—once ... twice—and the door popped open.

Thurman stood at the front door, fumbling with the lock, and cast a panicked look over his shoulder at Adam. He got the lock undone and was opening the door as Adam reached him.

Adam, wanting to avoid manhandling the much smaller ranger, stiff-armed the door closed.

Thurman yelped, then took off back down the hall toward the kitchen. Just as he reached the end of the hall, Ann appeared in the doorway.

Thurman barreled into her, and she fell back into the kitchen with a cry.

As Adam raced down the hallway, he heard muffled thumps. When he reached the kitchen, he found Ann on the floor, arms wrapped around Thurman's ankle, and Thurman, notwithstanding this impediment, trying to make his way to the back door.

Adam grabbed his arm.

"You have him?" Ann asked, her voice muffled.

"Yes."

Ann released Thurman's ankle and climbed to her feet.

"Thanks," said Adam.

"Don't mention it," she said, brushing at the seat of her pants.

"Thurman," said Adam, "we're going to sit down and you're going to explain why you ran away. And if you try it again, I'm going to catch you and cuff you and drive you to the station, and we'll have the conversation in an interrogation room. Are we clear?"

Thurman's shoulders slumped. "Yes."

Adam pointed to one of the benches. "Sit."

Thurman sat.

Ann dropped onto the bench opposite Thurman. "You're

not going to call in reinforcements?" she asked Adam, a bit winded.

Adam leaned against the wall near the door and crossed his arms. "Not yet. I want to talk to him first myself." He rattled off the Miranda warning. Then, casting an appraising eye over the ranger, he said, "Thurman, I hope you don't mind me saying so, but I just can't picture you administering the beating Bill Brackney got."

"I didn't!" squeaked Thurman.

"But Priscilla here," he gestured to the space next to Thurman, where Ann had directed her attention during the conversation with the spirit, "tells us you were here that night."

"Actually," said Ann to Adam, "she's standing next to you now."

Adam glanced to his right.

"Other side," Ann clarified.

He resisted glancing to his left.

"You're taking the word of a woman who claims to talk with ghosts?" asked Thurman. He scanned the area around Adam nervously.

"You had a pretty dramatic reaction to what you're now claiming was some kind of trumped-up séance," said Adam. "I must admit I was a skeptic at first, but you running when Ann said your name ..." He shook his head. "... that was enough to convince me."

Adam couldn't help noticing Ann's satisfied smile.

"I just got nervous," said Thurman, "being in the house after hours with a crazy woman. You can't use that as evidence."

"Maybe not, but now that Ann has told me what happened—"

"Priscilla," corrected Ann.

"Now that *Priscilla* has told us what happened," amended

Adam, "I'll take an extra careful look at your appearance at Germantown Friends School that night. After all, it's only a two-minute walk. You could easily have slipped out during a break and run back here for a few minutes."

"I was the main speaker. I couldn't have run out, killed someone, and run back without anyone noticing!"

"I agree. Like I said, I don't see you being the killer. But you could have unlocked the door and left again."

Thurman crossed his arms and fixed his eyes on the tabletop. "I want a lawyer."

Adam sighed. "I think that's a very good idea."

"We didn't hear everything Priscilla had to say," said Ann. She looked a few feet to Adam's left. "Priscilla, do you have more to tell us?" Ann was silent for half a minute, then shifted her gaze to Adam. "She says the killer was someone named Nicky."

Adam's eyebrows rose. "Nicky Rinaldi? He was the carpenter that Bill fired."

"I didn't think he was going to kill him!" blurted Thurman. "Nicky said he just wanted to talk to Bill about why he fired him, but that Bill wouldn't meet with him on the site during the day."

"Thurman," cautioned Adam, "I think your first instinct to wait to talk until you have a lawyer was a smart one."

"But it's the truth—I thought he just wanted to talk to him!" Thurman looked down at his hands. "Nicky's a good guy. I didn't think anything bad would happen."

"I believe you, but my advice stands. And I think we'll have to have that conversation at the station, after all." Adam turned to Ann. "And as soon as we get Thurman bundled off to the station, I want to hear the rest of Priscilla's story."

Ann nodded. "We'll be here."

❦

Half an hour later, Adam turned Thurman over to a pair of uniforms accompanied by a Park Service ranger.

As he walked down the hall toward the kitchen, he could hear Ann's voice, a pause, and then her laugh.

He stepped into the room, and she turned, still smiling.

"What's up?" he asked.

"Priscilla was just telling me some of the things she's seen at the house." Ann must have noticed Adam's raised eyebrows because she added, "Nothing else illegal. Or at least nothing worth your attention." She shook her head. "It's not until you hear someone from another time talk about your own time that you realize how weird some things are."

Adam feared that if he asked what those things were, he might be here for quite a while. "Where is she now?" he asked, scanning the room.

Ann gestured toward the bench opposite where she sat.

Adam started to lower himself onto the bench next to Ann.

She gestured again toward the opposite bench. "I think Priscilla would like it if you sat next to her," she said with an amused smile.

He hesitated, then circled the table. He pointed to the end of the bench. "Here?" He had no desire to sit on Priscilla.

Ann nodded.

He sat and turned toward the seemingly empty space next to him. "I'd love to hear the rest of your story, Priscilla."

Priscilla reached the kitchen, still wondering who other than the girls would arrive for a late-night visit to Bill. She found Bill standing on one side of the table and a man she recognized as one of the workers—she had heard the men call him Nicky—on the other. She hadn't seen Nicky at the house for some time.

"*You seem awful goddamned worked up about a lost job,*" *Bill was saying. "From what I hear, you've got plenty of other work—it's not like you're going to go hungry.*"

"*It's not you firing me I'm worked up about,*" *Nicky shot back, his face red. "It's the reason you fired me.*"

"*There wasn't enough work to keep you on. I like you, Nicky, but I can't invent work to keep you on the payroll—*"

"*That's bullshit. You just didn't want me around reminding you about what you did to my sister.*"

Bill paled. "What do you mean?"

"*Don't pretend like you don't know what I'm talking about,*" *Nicky said through clenched teeth. "You met her that day I brought her by—she was so excited to get to walk through the house while it was closed to the public for the renovation—and I saw how you looked at her.*"

Bill shrugged, affecting nonchalance. "She's a good-looking girl. Doesn't mean I did anything to her."

"*From what I hear, you don't make much of a distinction between seeing something you like and doing something about it. And girl is exactly what she was. She was sixteen years old, for God's sake.*"

"*How would I know how old she was?*"

"*You didn't bother asking?*"

"*Why would I?*"

"*Because she's a minor. Because you having your way with her broke the law. Although maybe you care as little about breaking the law as about breaking someone's heart.*"

Bill dropped his head. The pose might have suggested shame, but from where Priscilla stood, she could see that Bill was trying to hide a smirk.

Nicky wasn't fooled. He stepped around the table and Bill's head snapped up, his smirk gone.

"*You broke her heart,*" *Nicky repeated, his voice trembling. "You killed her as surely as if you had pushed her off the bridge.*"

"What makes you think it had anything to do with me?" said Bill, trying to imbue his words with self-righteous indignation.

"She told me."

Bill took a few seconds to regroup, then heaved a dramatic sigh. "Okay, fine. But it was her that came on to me. And," he added with a bit of a whine in his tone, "she told me it all had to be hush-hush. So then she rushed home and told brother Nicky all about it?"

Nicky's face went from red to white, and when he spoke, his voice was deadly cold. "She never told anyone—at least not before she died. Want to know how I know?"

Bill's eyes widened, and he took a step backwards.

Nicky took a step forward. "Not curious, Bill?"

After a long pause, Bill said reluctantly, "Yeah, sure. Why not."

"I'll have to show you. Follow me."

"Where?"

"Upstairs."

Bill's features relaxed fractionally. "Okay, fine."

Nicky gestured toward the hallway. "After you."

Bill glanced speculatively at the back door. Priscilla could see that it was locked, and Nicky could surely catch Bill before he could get it unlocked. Bill must have come to the same conclusion because he shook his head, walked past Nicky, and started down the hall. Nicky followed. Priscilla trailed them up the stairs.

When they reached the second-floor landing, Nicky gestured toward the back bedroom. "In there."

Bill looked like he might be regretting having agreed to Nicky's invitation. He walked down the hallway and stepped into the room, positioning himself next to the open door. Nicky brushed past him and crossed to the other side of the room. Priscilla, in the hallway just outside, could sense Bill's demeanor relax fractionally. After all, as far as he was concerned, there was nothing standing between him and a flight down the steps if need be.

"So," said Bill, glancing around the room, "you wanted to show me something."

"I wanted to tell you something first—about how I know about you and Evie." Nicky pulled an envelope—light pink and decorated with a butterfly in one corner—from his pocket and held it up. "She told me in her suicide note. She left it where no one but me would find it. She begged me not to tell our mom or her dad. She knew it would kill them, just like it killed her, to know what you did to her. She only told me."

Bill drew himself up. "And, what, she told you to bring me up here and rough me up?"

Nicky turned and put the envelope on the mantle. "No, she was too good a person for that."

Bill's smirk returned, and in a bit of bravado that he would no doubt regret for the short remainder of his life, he said, "Not that good."

With a roar, Nicky snatched up the poker leaning against the fireplace and wheeled on Bill.

Bill's smirk disappeared, and he spun and lunged for the door.

Nicky was several strides away, and Bill might have made it down the stairs and out the door to the relative safety of Germantown Avenue. But when he stepped into the space occupied by Priscilla, he recoiled with a shudder, and in that second Nicky caught up with him, grabbed his arm, spun him around, and swung the poker.

The first blow caught Bill on the side of the head before he could shout, but not before Priscilla screamed.

She staggered back into the hall and watched, horrified, as Nicky swung the poker again, this time catching Bill in the face.

She slapped her hand over her eyes and backed down the hallway, wondering vaguely if she would be injured if she misjudged her position and stepped blindly into the stairwell. When her back hit the wall at the other end of the hall, she slid to the floor and wrapped her arms around her head, trying to block not only the sight of Nicky's attack on Bill, but its sounds as well.

It seemed an eternity, but was probably less than a minute, when the thumps of the blows and the grunts and gasps of their recipient fell silent, and the only sound Priscilla heard was her own shuddering sobs and Nicky's panting breath.

She raised her eyes.

Nicky was bent over Bill's prone form, one hand supporting himself on his knee, the other holding the poker. A minute ticked by, and his breathing gradually slowed. Finally, he straightened, his movements those of an old man. He picked up the envelope from the mantle and went to the body. The poker dropped from his hand.

He bent and grasped the heavy gold necklace that hung around Bill's neck and, with a violence that made Priscilla flinch, yanked it off. He straightened and dropped the necklace into the envelope, then bent over the body again, holding the envelope in front of Bill Brackney's sightless eyes.

"I'm going to take this to Holy Sepulchre," Nicky hissed, "and I'm going to bury it at Evie's grave so she'll know that I made you pay."

As if on autopilot, he picked up the poker and stepped over the body and out of the room. He staggered down the hallway toward Priscilla, and she pulled herself into a ball, although she knew she had nothing to fear from him.

He made his way down the steps, the bloody poker leaving a trail of droplets in his wake.

ANN RELAYED Priscilla's story to Adam as the young woman told it. When Priscilla finished, her eyes on her hands clenched white-knuckled in her lap, Ann asked, "What's Holy Sepulchre? A church?"

"It's a cemetery," said Adam, "about fifteen minutes north of here. But who the hell is Evie?" He drummed his fingers on the table for a moment, then was still. "Wait a minute … are we talking about Evelyn Barone?"

"Who is Evelyn Barone?"

"A sixteen-year-old who jumped off the Walnut Street Bridge into the Schuylkill. Bystanders pulled her out but couldn't revive her." He drew his phone from his pocket and tapped for a minute, then heaved a sigh. "Goddamn. Nicholas Rinaldi's mother's last name is Barone. She must have gotten remarried after Nicky was born, changed her name, and then Evelyn—Evie—came along." He looked at Ann, his eyes weary. "Nicky Rinaldi was Evie Barone's half-brother."

"And when Nicky Rinaldi killed Bill, he was avenging Evie."

"That's what I'm thinking."

"And since Nicky worked at Whistler-Talbot House before Bill fired him, he knew the poker would be in the bedroom. It wasn't a weapon of convenience. It was all planned out." After a pause, she added, "He even brought his sister's suicide note with him."

"Yeah."

"I wonder where the poker is now."

"If Nicky Rinaldi believed in poetic justice—and it looks like he did—I'm betting it's at the bottom of the Schuylkill." Adam stood. "I'm going up to Holy Sepulchre and see if I can find the chain at Evelyn Barone's grave. If it's there and if it has Rinaldi's fingerprints on it, that should give us what we need to arrest him, or at least bring him in for another round of questioning." He looked in the general direction of where Priscilla stood. "Thank you, Priscilla—you've been a big help."

Priscilla blushed a deep red, and a pleased smile played at her lips.

Adam turned to Ann. "You coming?"

"I'll catch up with you in a minute," said Ann.

He nodded and left the room.

"What happens now?" asked Priscilla. "Will Thurman and

Nicky be hanged?"

"No, we don't do that anymore," said Ann. "But if Adam can find evidence that will back up what you say, he can make sure Nicky Rinaldi goes to prison." She sighed. "It's too bad we can't call you as a witness."

"But *you* could tell the court what happened."

Ann smiled ruefully. "I'm afraid the authorities wouldn't take anything I told them seriously … and even if they did, it would be inadmissible in court. But now that Adam knows what you saw, it will be a big help to him in putting together a case."

"You can take the credit," Priscilla said gamely. "Maybe he'll be so grateful that—"

Ann raised her hand. "Priscilla, I know you're trying to be helpful, but let's not go there."

Priscilla raised her eyebrows. "Go where?"

Ann laughed. "Let's not go down that path." She stood. "I'll let you know what happens. Thanks again for your help."

Priscilla listened to Ann's footsteps retreat down the hall and, a moment, later, heard the front door close behind her.

Let's not go there? It wasn't only twenty-first century courtship Priscilla didn't understand.

She wandered down the hall to the front room and the windows overlooking the street. Ann and Adam stood on the sidewalk, talking, then shook hands and headed in opposite directions. Priscilla herself would have found an excuse to follow Adam, and he seemed enough of a gentleman to pretend he believed it.

But she knew she would never leave the house.

She didn't mind, now that it was her *house. And it was better without Bill Brackney waiting in the kitchen for a visitor. She turned from the window.*

But once Adam found the necklace, perhaps not better for Nicky Rinaldi, who had only wanted to see his sister avenged.

~

IF YOU ENJOYED *this Ann Kinnear and Adam Kaminski Suspense Short, check out Ann and Adam's novel-length adventures: Ann's by Matty Dalrymple (https://www.mattydalrymple.com/) and Adam's by Jane Gorman (https://www.janegorman.com/index.html)*

MATTY DALRYMPLE IS the author of the Lizzy Ballard Thrillers, beginning with ROCK PAPER SCISSORS; the Ann Kinnear Suspense Novels, beginning with THE SENSE OF DEATH; and the Ann Kinnear Suspense Shorts. She is a member of International Thriller Writers and Sisters in Crime. Matty also writes, speaks, and consults on the writing craft and the publishing voyage, and shares what she's learned on THE INDY AUTHOR PODCAST. She has written books on the business of short fiction and podcasting for authors; her articles have appeared in Writer's Digest magazine. She is a member of the Alliance of Independent Authors.

JANE GORMAN IS the author of the Adam Kaminski Mysteries, beginning with A BLIND EYE, and the Cape May Cozy Mysteries with a Twist, beginning with SCONES AND SCOFFLAWS. Before turning her attention to mystery, Jane worked briefly in academia after completing a doctorate in Cultural Anthropology, then shifted gears to become a diplomat with the U.S. Department of State. Jane is a member of Sisters in Crime.

BE STILL MY HEART

JANIS WILSON

No one would have expected them to hook up. Tony Pennington was six feet four and Marsha Chen, with her lovely almond eyes and petite form, was under five feet. The hardened newspaper staff couldn't help smiling when thinking about them.

Sure, there had been affairs at the paper. Young people are drawn to journalism and bring with them hormones and romantic notions. But this had been different. It was clear they would become one and they gained the nickname "Chennington."

Tony's proposal wasn't the stuff of romance novels. He expected an immediate acceptance, but she was a Jane Austen fan. He wasn't rebuffed as harshly as Elizabeth Bennett had spurned Mr. Darcy, but he did meet with opposition.

"We have nothing in common," Marsha said. "You're from the Midwest; I grew up in the South. I'm an animal lover; you're a hunter."

"Yes, and I'm a runner but you suck wind walking up the

stairs. But we're both reporters who worship the almighty scoop. We're great together. Besides, opposites attract."

"This opposite isn't attracted to someone who blows holes in animals."

"You eat meat," Tony countered.

"Exactly. You shouldn't marry a hypocrite."

Tony laughed and hugged her. "We can work things out."

"All right. We can get married, but I don't want you using that gun," Marsha said.

"I go hunting every season with my dad. You know that."

"It creeps me out. I imagine bloody bodies every time I see it."

"Okay. I'll sell it at a gun show next fall," he promised.

"You would do that?" she asked.

"I love you. I even love how much you hate my shotgun. I love how you tap your chest and say, 'Be still my heart,' whenever you get a good assignment or catch some politician in a lie."

After that romantic speech, Marsha had to accept. They spent the rest of the evening planning the wedding they'd have to pay for and drafting their wedding vows. Romantic but feminist, Marsha would never consent to being "given away," though she loved and revered her parents.

Invitations went out six months after the couple met. Marsha was proud of her heritage and chose not to take Tony's name. Tony was fine with that.

On their honeymoon, Tony unexpectedly began to feel pain so severe the couple came home early. Having paid for a wedding, Tony wasn't looking to spend another dime, but he couldn't work with the pain and nausea. The doctor diagnosed a kidney stone, promising it would pass on its own. When the nausea became debilitating, Tony begged for stronger medicine. It didn't help, so he found a specialist.

"You've got to give me something," Tony told the nephrologist. "My head swims and I puke a lot."

"Nausea and kidney stones go together," the doctor said. "Compazine will help." He wrote a prescription.

Tony quickly filled the prescription and gulped down the pills with greedy anticipation. "They make me so sleepy I can't function, honey," he told Marsha. Worse than the pain, he was having difficulty making love. He'd rather vomit every day than forego sex.

Tony returned to Dr. Morley, whose office was on Rose Tree Road, which was happily situated a few miles from the newsroom. "I can't stand being impotent and my wife deserves better, God knows. But I'm dizzy and can barely stay awake. Are you sure you gave me the right medicine?"

The doctor plucked his prescription pad from a desk drawer and wrote new orders, replacing the Compazine with Ondansetron. "Dissolve it under your tongue. It will make you instantly sleepy, so only use it at home."

Tony filled the prescription immediately. He put a tablet under his tongue and felt better faster than he could wink. When he entered the newsroom the next day, his editor said, "I thought you were supposed to stay home."

"Yeah, but I've got that press conference," Tony said. When he got to City Hall, he was still drowsy. He tried jiggling his leg up and down. He rubbed his face. Nothing seemed to invigorate him. Only when other reporters began shouting questions at the mayor did Tony realize he'd been nearly unconscious.

"You've got to take time off," Marsha insisted. "Your pain is so bad you can't work, and you can't cover a story if you're sound asleep."

Tony followed his wife's instructions and soon felt better. The kidney pain and the nausea lessened.

To celebrate Tony's improved health, the couple treated

themselves to dinner at the Wok and Roll, around the corner from the paper. Tony, never daring in the culinary sense, stuck with pork fried rice. The adventurous Marsha, impressed by the French name, ordered Caneton de Rouen à la Press.

"Are you sure that's a good idea in a place like this?" Tony asked.

"I've wanted to try it ever since I saw that duck press in the window of La Fourchette D'Or. And we're not likely to be eating there any time soon. You know I love to try new things," she said. After the first forkful, she pronounced the entrée delicious and cleaned her plate.

At home that night, the couple snuggled but Tony's pain returned. That didn't explain why Marsha was sick, too. She realized the duck had been a poor choice. If she wasn't sure, she soon had proof by duck repeatedly reappearing for her inspection.

The ailing newlyweds rejoiced at having each other to help them through this difficult time. Tony had taken the familiar "in sickness and in health" vow but never gave it any thought until now.

Severe pain woke Tony, who found Marsha hugging the toilet. Although he was suffering, he attended to Marsha. Selflessly, she said, "Take your medicine first," she said. "You can't really help me until you do."

Tony dissolved a tablet under his tongue and recovered in an instant. His relief from pain and nausea approximated euphoria but he awoke at around 3 a.m. to the sound of retching. He couldn't bear to see Marsha sick and weak.

"I've never been so sick in my life," Marsha said. "It must have been that freaking duck. Maybe some of its blood got in the meat. The chef crushes the bones, you know. I took Pepto Bismol, but I puked it up, too."

"I'll call an ambulance," Tony said.

"No, I'm not that sick. I'll be okay now that I've vomited practically the whole bird out of my system. I just wish I'd gotten drunk tonight. Then I would deserve how I feel."

"You don't deserve anything like this, sweetie," Tony comforted. "What can I do now?"

"Only death will help at this point," Marsha said.

"How about one of my nausea pills? They help me right away."

"Oh, God, yes. I hadn't thought of that. Let me have 'em. I'm dying here."

Tony pulled out the tablets that had given him such peace. "Put it under your tongue."

Marsha popped the pill into her mouth. In minutes, she breathed a deep sigh. "That really helped. I may actually survive."

Tony carried her to bed and kissed her forehead. "Don't put your arms around me," Marsha warned. "I may have to run to the toilet again."

"Let me know if you need me."

"I'll always need you, Tony" she said and smiled.

The couple settled back into the bed. Tony held Marsha's hand because it was the least intrusive comfort he could provide. Marsha fell asleep quickly but in about an hour she woke again soaked in sweat. "Give me another pill, honey," Marsha said. "At least I can get another hour's rest."

When the alarm went off, Tony asked, "How are you feeling, honey? Want me to stay home with you?" She didn't answer. Her forehead felt cooler than the previous evening. She didn't wake. He shouted but wasn't getting through. When he shook Marsha's shoulder, her head rolled to one side, but her eyes didn't open.

Panicked, he jumped from the bed and dialed 9-1-1. "I need an ambulance quick," he shouted, followed by the address. "Get here as fast as you can." He left the bed, slipped on a robe, and ran to the front door. After what seemed like an hour, there was a knock. Tony led the paramedics into the bedroom.

In less than a minute, one paramedic asked, "What's she been taking?"

"What do you mean?"

Exasperated, the man demanded, "What is she on, for God's sake?" The man wearing a white tunic with a "Delaware County Ambulance Service" shoulder patch bent over the unresponsive woman. "Oh, shit," he exclaimed.

"Hurry up, damn you," Tony shouted. "I'll help you get her on the gurney." He moved to the side of the bed but was halted by the annoyed paramedic whose partner was lifting the feather-light young woman from the bed. "Can you save her?' Tony asked.

"Sorry, bro, she's gone."

Tony was immobile, struggling to understand.

The younger paramedic placed the tiny woman on the gurney and pulled a sheet over her face. His supervisor pulled it back down and said, "Call the cops. We don't pronounce them."

"We don't need cops," Tony snapped. "She needs a doctor. Put her in the ambulance, for God's sake. Help her! Hurry up!" Tony said, tears falling down his cheeks.

The first paramedic grasped his arm and moved him away from the bed.

"Listen, man, she's gone," the paramedic said. "She's probably been dead for hours. We have to wait for the coroner. I'm sorry, bro. You might want someone to come and stay with you."

Tony realized the man was offering comfort, but it did no good. His mind was blank, but his loss was palpable.

The coroner arrived, listened for a heartbeat, and pulled the sheet over her face. "Take her away," he said. Sensitive to the grieving young man, he chose his words cautiously. He told the ambulance crew, "you know where she's going."

Tony knew the unspoken word was "morgue." He sat on the bed, unable to move. Finally, he rose, his knees wobbly. He needed to tell his boss he wouldn't be coming to work that day. Tompkins, the city editor, answered.

"I'm not coming in today," Tony said.

"So, I'm guessing the bride will be staying home all day today, too," the editor joked.

"What do you mean?" Tony stammered, uncomprehending.

"Marsha isn't in yet. Is she going to be late?"

Reporters are taught to use precise words and to avoid euphemisms. "She's dead," Tony said.

Tompkins didn't get the bad joke. "What are you talking about?"

"She's dead. She ate rotten food, and it killed her. The ambulance just left."

Tompkins was reluctant to play along. If this was a joke, it was in unforgivably bad taste, even for a reporter. He questioned Tony about the cause of the tragedy.

"Where are you?"

"Apartment," Tony said.

"Sit tight. I'll have someone get to you. Do you understand, Tony?"

"I'm never going to understand," he said and hung up.

Tompkins scanned the newsroom. He needed someone level-headed who wasn't on deadline. He knew Mark was a pal of Tony's.

"Stewart, get over here."

Tompkins relayed the new information. "If that restaurant's food killed Marsha, it's a page one story. Check with the D.A. If they're filing charges, give me something for the first edition tomorrow. Then go check on Tony. I don't want him to be alone. See if there's anything he needs. Check with the cop shop and see if they know anything. If they don't, you'll have to tell them about Marsha. Tony's not thinking straight. Don't worry about coming back today. Do whatever you can to help him. Let me know how he is."

"Sure thing." Mark said. Acting on years of experience, he walked to the vending machine and bought a protein bar. He might not eat for the rest of the day unless he could persuade Tony to join him, but the guy was about to bury his bride. He wouldn't have an appetite.

Mark knocked on the front door, then tried his phone to see how long it would take Tony to answer. It wasn't long before Tony opened the door. "I just heard," Mark said. "I'm so sorry."

Tony broke all the reporters' rules of aloofness and threw his arms around Mark, who gave him a slap on the back and led him into the apartment. The two men sat and Tony, answering Mark's precise questions, relayed the full story.

Mark pressed for details.

"Dude, you know what happened," Tony said. "That crappy restaurant served a rotten duck. Why do you think a place with a comic book name would suddenly offer a dish with a fancy French name?"

Meanwhile, Mark called his sources and learned Marsha's body was transferred to the Medical Examiner. He shared this information with Tony.

"Why would they do that to her? I don't want my wife sliced up on some cold, aluminum table."

A few days later, Tony managed to suit up and walk into the newsroom. People pumped his hand or gave him a kiss. Tony hadn't expected such treatment by hardened newshounds. They had really loved Marsha.

"Want to get some lunch?" Mark asked later.

"Thanks, but I've got to get to the Wok and see who killed my wife."

Tony walked into the restaurant and was greeted by a polite, middle-aged man. "I want to know where you bought that fancy French duck you served a couple of days ago," he said.

"I'm so glad you enjoyed it," the unsuspecting host said.

"Haven't the police told you? You killed my wife!"

The host grew pale and began stammering that he knew nothing about his wife. "I want to see the owner this minute," Tony said.

"I am Charlie Bao. This is my restaurant. There is never anything wrong with the food."

"We ate here the night you served that poison duck," Tony shouted. "It was so special my wife died of food poisoning the next day. I can't believe the health department hasn't shut you down yet."

Bao tried to quiet the loud young man or to push him through the front door before he disturbed the diners. "I don't know what you're talking about. Please quiet down. People will get upset."

"Wait until one of them dies of salmonella or whatever bacteria are seasoning your food. That'll upset them for sure," Tony said.

"If you don't leave, I'll call the police."

"Good. It is about time they got here."

"You go now," Bao said, and Tony realized nothing could be accomplished by his ranting. He wanted Bao in jail but his temper tantrum wasn't going to accomplish that. He left and went to talk to people he knew could help him.

The next day, Tony didn't show up for work. The police scanner broadcast news of a hostage situation at a local bank. Tony had reported on hostage takings, making him the perfect reporter to cover the story.

"Mark," the city editor called. "Come here."

Mark walked over.

"Seen Tony?" the editor asked.

"Not since yesterday."

Tompkins scratched his beard. "I don't like it. Why would he come here the first part of the week and then suddenly stop coming to work?"

"He might need some more time. You know, to cry it out, maybe," Mark said.

"He hasn't called in and that's not like him," the city editor said. "Do me a favor. Get over to his place and check on him."

"I'm sure it is nothing," Mark said with a shrug. "I thought you wanted me for the hostage thing." One could hear the disappointment in his voice.

"Anybody can cover breaking news," Tompkins said. "Right now, we need to follow up on the Marsha story. Tony wants somebody arrested for her death. Says the restaurant is guilty of manslaughter. Check with the cops. Then go see the district attorney. We need to know if there's anything to support Tony's theory about Marsha being served spoiled food. After you talk to the D.A., go check on Tony. Call me soon as you can."

Mark walked to the courthouse and asked for the prosecutor handling Marsha's case. He assumed Tony had reported the restaurant for serving tainted food. Mark was referred to the most junior deputy D.A. in the office, Greg Atkinson.

It was an election year, making the district attorney sensitive to press inquiries. When he found out there were allegations that rotten food had killed a popular young reporter, he knew the paper would be gunning for the restaurant. As soon as he heard the allegations, the district attorney ordered a deputy to open a file on Marsha's case. He doubted the truth of the allegation. People just don't die of food poisoning anymore. So, he assigned the matter to a rookie.

Atkinson was so junior he hadn't yet received the results of his bar exam. That meant he was routinely assigned all the nuisance cases. But this case, while a headache, could boost his career. If he could get the press off the D.A.'s back, Atkinson would be noticed and, possibly, rewarded for his diligence.

Mark told Atkinson the sad story. Marsha's body had been sent to the Medical Examiner and an autopsy performed. Atkinson pulled the file himself and skimmed it while Mark asked questions.

"What was the cause of death?" Mark asked.

Atkinson studied the autopsy report. "Heart attack, apparently."

"What? She was young and healthy."

Atkinson didn't lift his eyes from the report. "Turns out she had some condition she might not even have known about."

"Like what?"

"Something called Brugada Syndrome. It leaves fatty deposits in the heart."

"But she was a tiny little thing," Mark observed. "She didn't have an ounce of fat on her anywhere."

Atkinson shrugged. "Beats me. I'm just telling you what it says here," indicating the file. "She took drugs that she shouldn't have. They're what killed her."

"What the hell are you talking about?" Mark snapped. "Believe me, Marsha wasn't on drugs." Mark thought if the M.E. had botched this autopsy there would be a story in it.

The young prosecutor shook his head. "Wasn't like that," he said. "They only found prescription drugs in her system. Something called Ondansetron."

"Which is what?" Mark leaned forward, excited by this information so uncharacteristic of Marsha.

"Ondansetron is something to prevent nausea. They give it to people on chemo."

Marked balled up his fists. "Are you sure you have the right file? She wasn't on chemo. Who would have prescribed that stuff for her?"

"That's interesting," Atkinson said. "We couldn't trace that prescription to any of her doctors. CVS had no record of it."

"Then she didn't have food poisoning?" Mark asked. "You're not going to arrest anyone?"

"No reason to. We just got the autopsy report. The M.E. said she never should have taken the nausea medicine. It caused some kind of reaction because she had this weird condition. It was this drug that did her in, not anything she ate," Pointing to the report, Atkinson added, "Coroner says there was some kind of heart congestion. The blood couldn't get through the ventricle or something. The medicine messed up her heart rhythm."

"Are you even going to investigate the Chinese restaurant?"

"What for? The M.E ruled natural causes. She was already sick, but she probably wouldn't have known it for a day or two. Her intestinal lining tested positive for rotovirus. Only good news is she probably died in her sleep. Look, I don't know what your paper is trying to pull. I told all this to that other reporter."

Mark's lips tightened. "What reporter? I'd better not be getting scooped on a story involving a *Chronicle* reporter."

"You think we're so stupid? We wouldn't give a story about one of your staff to a competing paper. I told this to a reporter from the *Chronicle.*"

Mark was pissed. Why would the boss send someone else interview the D.A.?

"What was his angle?" Mark asked.

"He was asking about a manslaughter story," Atkinson said. "He acted really funny when I said it was the nausea medicine that killed her. That guy must really hate to lose out on a story. You should have seen his face."

"What was his name? Was he a big guy?" Mark asked and Atkinson nodded.

"Yeah." Atkinson glanced back at the file and said, "Called himself Pennington. I know he's one of your guys because I've seen his byline."

Mark swallowed hard. "Pennington was Marsha's husband."

The color drained from Atkinson's face. "Didn't know that," the deputy admitted and shrugged. "Different last name. But that explains why he took it so badly."

Without stopping to thank Atkinson, Mark rose and dashed out the door. With the cops unable to trace the medicine to Marsha's doctor, there was only one place she could have gotten it. It had to have been Tony's medicine. And Atkinson had just dropped this information on Tony like a bomb. Tony would need comfort now more than ever. Then he remembered Tony's recent stomach troubles. Mark had to find out if this Ondansetron was prescribed for Tony. But that could wait.

Feeling panicky, Mark ran to Tony's first floor apartment. He hammered on the door. No answer. Maybe he just wanted to be alone. Too bad. Mark had to see him. He went to the window and shaded his eyes against the glare before stumbling backward. He called the cops.

"Stay outside," said one officer. But he was talking to a reporter, and they don't take kindly to being kept away from a story.

"He's my friend," Mark said, disregarding their instructions and pushing in. Sure enough, Tony had put things together. It was he, not some smelly duck, who had killed Marsha. Running into the bedroom, Mark was met with a chilling answer to the mystery.

Tony was sprawled across the bed. At his feet was his shotgun. On the wall were his brains.

Janis Wilson is the author of the Lady Sarah Grey mysteries. Her first novel was *Goulston Street, the Quest for Jack the Ripper.* Her soon-to-be published second novel delves into the poisoning death of Karl Marx's youngest daughter. Ms. Wilson has published award-winning newspaper articles. A retired trial lawyer, she has written for and edited various legal publications. She is a frequent commentator on true crime programs such as "Snapped: Killer Couples," "Nightmare Next Door," and "Deadly Affairs." Her website is JanisWilson.com. She and her husband reside in the Philadelphia suburbs, where two rescue cats live under their protection.

THE CASE OF THE LOST LHASA

DOUGLAS GAINES HARRELL

"Lucy, where are you?" Colin, tall, dark, and frantic, was searching his beach rental for any sign of his little dog. He had just woken and had been startled not to find her at his feet. He dashed outside calling her name, only to realize he was dressed in the plaid boxers and ripped T-shirt he had slept in. Sheepishly slinking back inside, he tossed on shorts and sneakers, grabbed his keys, and ran out of the house.

AT PET-FRIENDLY BOW-MEOW Books in Rehoboth Beach, Delaware, it was a lazy August morning. The four-legged staff, all rescues, were amusing themselves by testing their powers of observation on the early customers. Sherlock, a rare dun-brown whippet, was a master of deduction with a keen nose. His faithful companion, Watson, was an all-white bull terrier. Watson was not clever, but he was stout of heart and could always be counted on for muscle. Hercule was Sherlock's equal in brains but was prone to distraction when grooming. He was a fastidious grey Persian with a white mustache and tummy. Lastly, Jane was an older calico of no pedigree. Her specialty was observing how a person or animal behaved to determine their psychology. She had honed this skill living for years among a community of barn cats in Fort Meade, Maryland.

Watson began the analysis. "I say he's a dog's human."

"Why do you say that?" Jane asked, as the athletic, young man walked directly toward the front desk and got in line. "He has a gentle poise. Notice how gracefully he walks."

"He reminds me of my old human," said Watson.

"Not very scientific, old friend," said Sherlock. "Single men are more likely to favor dogs, and I observe the absence of a wedding ring. Not all married men wear rings, but I think we can safely assume he is single, as any wife would have long ago discarded that tattered garment he's wearing."

"I say he's a dog's human based on what appears to be a long, white hair clinging to his derriere," said Hercule. "We cats have fur, not hair, and any self-respecting cat would have deposited much more fur on his human than that."

"Still," observed Sherlock, "there's no substitute for a good sniff." With that, he walked over and put his head near the man's leg and shoes. Returning after a pat and a scratch, he declared, "Definitely a dog's man. His dog is a female, and he feeds her a grain-free, small-breed formula with tuna. The little Maltese in the cage next to me used to eat something similar. I hate that smell. It reminds me of the shelter."

"How on earth do you know what she eats just by smelling her human's shoes?" asked Watson.

"She drools—probably naps on them," answered Sherlock. "From his scent, I can also tell the man ate sausage pizza from Spicoli's recently. I've made a study of food smells, and Spicoli's sausage is unique in Rehoboth for its use of Jamaican allspice. My old human used to take me tracking. I won every competition save one. Lost to a setter named Irish Adelaide, a remarkable female. Out of respect, she will always be known to me as "The Bitch."

Jane tried to predict the man's preference in books. "I'm having a hard time getting a read on him. He just seems upset. Maybe self-help, but I wouldn't bet on it."

"I did smell adrenaline," said Sherlock.

When the man's turn came for his "audience" with the owners of the store, "Her Majesties Victoria and Regina, the Empresses of India Ink," as they were known to their animal subjects, he put his hands a foot apart and spoke quickly and nervously.

"Wow. That's a big book," said Watson.

"Non, mon ami. He is relating something about his little white companion," observed Hercule, in between licking his paw and grooming his mustache. "Given his agitation, I surmise they have been separated."

Sherlock leaped to attention. "A case! Watson, on your paws. The game is afoot!"

FOR THE REST of the morning, Jane assessed customers and animals, but didn't pick up anything useful. Sherlock gave everyone a good sniff for signs of the little white dog. Not finding any, he chewed his squeaky pipe to contemplate, while Hercule restored his "little gray furs" with a nap in the sunny windowsill. Watson had named their investigation "The Case of the Missing Maltese." He helped Sherlock until story time, when he had to go to work. Watson treated children suffering from a fear of dogs by sitting adorably as they read stories to him. He liked the petting, and the condition of his patients always improved.

Shortly before "high sun time," known to humans as

noon, they got a break in the case. A young woman with a beautiful coat of black head-hair came into the store followed by a small, white dog sporting a pink leash and collar covered in rhinestones. Jane correctly predicted the woman was headed for the "large human pectorals and mammaries" section. Sherlock went over to say hello. After they each got a good sniff, the little dog turned and pleaded, "Help me."

Sherlock recognized her scent immediately. "That woman is not your human."

"No. My human is lost. I got out this morning to go exploring and he hasn't caught up with me yet."

"Didn't your human provide you with tags?"

"Yes, of course, but they were attached to the most dreadful collar. I mean, if you'd seen it. The first thing I did was scrape it off against the corner of a building."

"Do not distress yourself. My colleagues and I will help you. Does your human eat sausage pizza and display questionable taste in his wardrobe?"

"That's him! Is he here?"

"No, but he was here this morning looking for you."

"Oh, thank DOG! I was afraid I would never see him again. I met this woman this morning. She's very nice, but I prefer a large male as pack leader. Still, she has a fabulous fashion sense. The first thing she did was take me shopping. I hope she'll let me keep this outfit."

Sherlock called his cohorts over. Hercule raised an eyelid and said he could hear fine from the windowsill.

"I am Sherlock. Allow me to present Watson and Jane. That is Hercule."

"Is this the missing Maltese we've been looking for?" Watson asked.

The little dog bristled. "Please. I'm a Lhasa apso. Maltese. I mean, *really!*"

"I forgot to ask your name," said Sherlock.

"Lucy, with my human. However, this woman is calling me–"

As if on cue, the woman took a few steps and gave a tug, "Katniss, over here, honey."

Sherlock said, "The problem is how to find your human. Do you know his name?"

"It sounds like 'Collar,' but I'm not sure. I call him Meal Ticket. I think her name is Walkies, but I only heard it once."

"Not very helpful. Can you describe the area where you last walked Collar?"

"Yes, there were lots of wooden houses with screen porches."

"That describes most of the town. Can you think of anything else?"

"On our walks, I saw a German shepherd, a golden retriever, and a tiny little dachshund."

"Shepherds and retrievers lead their humans on long walks," said Sherlock. "Even if we find them that doesn't narrow our search. But miniature dachshunds don't stray far from home. Can you describe him?"

"Oh, yes. He's very handsome. Black and brown with a long, luxurious coat. He'd be just my type if he weren't such a pussyfoot. He won't walk unless his human picks him up and carries him away from the house. Then he trots home ... looking *gorgeous*."

From the corner, Hercule perked up an ear. "Ah. No doubt you are referring to Monsieur Hartley, or 'One Way,' as he is known. He's a year-round resident and lives near the noisy place with screaming children and lights that spin at night."

"That's him!" Lucy said.

Just then, book in hand, Walkies made her way to the cash register, pulling Lucy behind her. As they were leaving the store, Lucy pleaded, "Oh, please hurry. The way Walkies has been wrinkling her nose makes me think she wants to give me a bath, and we hardly know each other!"

"Where does Walkies stay?" Jane called after her.

"We're on a street near—"

And with a tug of the leash, she was gone.

HERCULE JOINED Jane and Watson in a huddle around Sherlock as he spoke.

"We have two problems to solve. Where is Collar, and where is Walkies taking Lucy? Watson, you and I need to get onto Lucy's trail before it gets cold. Hercule and Jane, you go find Collar. Then we have to get them all back to the shop at the same time."

As Jane and Hercule made for the cat door, Sherlock went behind the counter with Watson close behind.

"Which one, Sherlock?" asked Watson.

"Regina, I think. She's easier to walk, and I see she's wearing her fang shoes today."

Watson began pushing at Regina's leg, while Sherlock pawed at the leashes hanging on the wall. Regina turned, and from her tone they could tell they had been successful.

Once outside, Regina made her usual turn to the right. Watson started to follow, but Sherlock stopped him. "Not that way, Watson. Our quarry went to the left." Watson stopped on the spot and waited for Regina to reach the end of her leash. Then he turned and began pulling her in the direction of the boardwalk. Teetering on her high heels, she had no choice but to follow.

When they reached the first cross street, the scent became even stronger. Sherlock followed it as far as Bash-er's but lost it in the maze of sweaty legs and squashed

French fries. Sitting down, he said, "I've lost the trail, Watson."

Watson sat next to him. Regina pulled on Watson's leash, but it might as well have been tied to a lamppost.

Thinking out loud, Watson said, "They can't have gone on the wooden street—no dogs allowed. And they can't have just disappeared."

"Watson, old boy, you've done it again. Once you eliminate the impossible, whatever remains, no matter how improbable, must be the truth. Lucy brought Walkies here to get fries, then doubled back. That's why the scent was stronger after we crossed the street."

They were off again, retracing their steps back to the corner, where they turned right. Little Regina was being dragged unsteadily behind Watson's sturdy gait as though she had harpooned a whale. Away from the big double street, with its heavy concentration of smells, it was a snap for Sherlock to follow the scent. After turning this way and that, the trail finally led up a front walk.

As they approached, Lucy gave a yelp from the screened in porch. "However did you find me?"

"Alimentary, my dear girl," said Sherlock. "You eat a lot of tuna fish."

As HE AND Jane went out the cat door to the alley, Hercule said, "Shall we proceed to the noisy place to find Monsieur One Way?"

Jane had the beginning of an idea, so she licked her paw to think. After a moment she said, "We could search, but I think I begin to understand Mr. Collar. It's almost 'high sun time,' and he does not have a female. Odds are good his refrigerator is empty, so he will need to find sustenance."

"Jane, my wise friend. You suggest we watch the dining establishments? A good thought, but there are so many. How will we choose?"

"He's dressed rather humbly for any of the finer restaurants, and I suspect he will want something he can eat while he continues his search."

"And we know he likes ze pizza," said Hercule.

"Spicoli's!" they said in unison and began racing in that direction. After agreeing on a plan, they took up positions on either side of the door. They didn't have to wait long before Jane spied Collar in his torn T-shirt.

"Hercule, he's coming."

"Mon Dieu! It is too soon. Our friends will need more time. We must wait before we act."

PER SHERLOCK'S INSTRUCTIONS, Watson marched up to the screen door, dragging Regina behind him. With his paw, he ripped open a gash large enough for Lucy to jump through. As soon as she was out, Sherlock bit his leash and pulled it out of Regina's hand. Then, Sherlock and Lucy took off running back toward the store. Watson, despite Regina's pulling and pleading, planted himself in front of the door and, doing his darndest to look mean, kept Walkies inside. Several bystanders tried to catch Lucy, but Sherlock moved in serpentine fashion around her as they ran. Once his two friends had a good head start, Watson turned around, yanked his leash out of Regina's hand, and sprinted back to the shop.

ABOUT THE TIME Collar entered Spicoli's, Jane and Hercule heard a commotion and turned to see the madcap chase on the opposite sidewalk: Sherlock clearing the way for Lucy, Watson close behind, and the two women hobbling after them a block behind. Time was now of the essence, and Jane and Hercule waited anxiously outside Spicoli's for Collar to exit.

Finally, Collar grabbed a bag and turned toward the door. Jane got into position, and just as Collar stepped out, she ran squarely into his legs and let out a convincing screech of pain. She lay there for a moment, feigning injury, and then slowly got up, holding out one of her front paws and limping.

As they had hoped, Collar made soothing sounds and bent down to read her tag. Then, he scooped her up in his free arm and began walking toward the store.

OUT OF BREATH AND FRANTIC, Regina and Walkies ran to the bookstore, where they were met at the door by store owner Victoria.

"Whatever happened? Sherlock and Watson just showed up barking at the door with this little, white dog."

A few feet inside the store, Sherlock was sitting up, looking regal as if nothing had happened, while several yards behind him, poor little Lucy was flat on her belly, panting furiously. Watson, also panting, had placed himself between Lucy and the door.

Stepping forward, Walkies exclaimed, "Katniss, thank goodness you're safe."

As she approached, Watson stood, showing his teeth and growling softly, stopping her in her tracks.

Regina ran over and grabbed Watson's collar. "Watson, what's gotten into you?" She then turned to Walkies. "Don't worry, he looks fearsome, but he's just a big puppy dog."

Regina tried to pull Watson toward his crate in the back of the store, but he stayed rooted to the spot.

"We are so sorry," said Victoria. "I can't imagine what's gotten into Sherlock and Watson, chasing your little dog like that."

"Thank you, but she's not mine. I wish she were. I found her wandering around lost this morning. She's so sweet I couldn't bring myself to take her to the shelter, so I called them and left my number. I bought this cute collar so I could walk her around and look for her owner."

"No luck, clearly. And no one called?"

"Someone may have. Like a dummy, I forgot to charge my phone last night and it died sometime this morning. I've had so much fun walking her around town that a part of me hopes no one ever calls."

"I don't blame you, but I think I know who her owner is. There was a guy here this morning looking for a little, white dog just before you came in. The way you've got her all blinged-out, I never imagined it could be the same dog."

Just then the door opened and in strutted Hercule. Behind him was Collar, with a paper bag in one hand and Jane draped over the other arm like a furry football. He saw Victoria and walked over.

"Hi, I'm Colin—I was in here earlier looking for my dog. I'm really sorry, but I stumbled over your cat. I think I hurt her paw."

Safely home, Jane hopped down and began rubbing against his leg with no sign of injury. Upon hearing her human's voice, Lucy let out a happy bark, and ran up to him wagging her tail.

"There you are, you rascal!" Colin got on one knee and set down the bag as Lucy jumped into his arms, licking his face profusely. "Where have you been girl, and where did you get that collar?" Then, he held her up out in front of him and said in his best Ricky Ricardo voice, "Lucy, you've got some 'splaining to do!" Standing, he asked, "Who do I have to thank for taking such good care of Lucy?"

A blushing Walkies shyly raised a gently waving hand. "That would be me. Hi, I'm Whitney."

Victoria politely excused herself and resumed her position behind the counter. Regina was busy rubbing Watson's tummy, as he had rolled over the moment Colin had come into the store.

"Thank you very much," said Colin. He returned Lucy to the floor, and she lay down with her head on Whitney's shoes. "She seems to like you."

"And I adore her. Such a sweetie pie. Honestly, I was hoping she was a stray so I could keep her."

"That's what I was afraid of. The shelter gave me a number, and I've been calling all morning, but no one ever picked up. I guess that was you."

"Yes, I'm sorry–my phone died."

"It happens. Excuse me a second. Let me get rid of this." Colin picked up the bag holding his uneaten takeout and walked over to a trash can. Then he walked back, smiling. "I'm kinda hungry. Can I buy you lunch as a thank-you?"

"That'd be great," said Whitney, running her hand through her hair. "Just let me go home first and change. I chased after Katniss—sorry, Lucy, for blocks. I must be a mess."

"If that's a mess, I can't wait to see you put together." He smiled and looked down. "Seems I could use a change, too."

"Shall we meet back here in an hour?"

"Sounds good. If there's any problem, I'll call you."

"And I'll answer this time!"

Lucy trotted over to Watson and licked his face. "My big, strong terrier." She seemed about to say more, but Colin picked her up, and carried her out of the store.

A FEW MINUTES LATER, with Jane on her perch by the door, and Hercule napping on the windowsill, Watson walked over to Sherlock.

"Well, Sherlock, another successful case."

"Thank you, Watson. I couldn't have done it without you."

"Your brains and my brawn, eh?"

"Precisely. But now I am again faced with the tedium of existence. Watson, I must have a case!"

"How about The Case of the Missing Milk-Bone?"

"You never tire of that one, do you, old friend? Very well."

They walked over to their queens, Victoria and Regina, and began pushing hard against their legs. Victoria held their collars while Regina took two treats and stalked out into the store looking for a good hiding place. Upon her return, Sherlock leaped to attention. "A case! Watson, on your paws. The game is afoot!"

DOUGLAS GAINES HARRELL is a recovering engineer who now writes full time in Wilmington, Delaware. In high school, he read about Sherlock Holmes, Dr. Watson, Hercule Poirot, and Jane Marple with a black cat named Midnight on his lap. Doug and his wife, Michelle, have been the humans of three wonderful orange tabby cats: Sherlock and Watson, who spent their long lives detecting food and warm laps, and Mr. Lemieux, who was too dignified to be called by his given name, Mario. They now live with their three orange tabby cats (are you sensing a pattern here?) Raymond, Robert, and Frankie who send their love to Aunt Jane and the other nice humans at Faithful Friends Animal Shelter who took such good care of them before they found their forever home. Visit Doug at www.douglasharrell.com.

133

"The Case of the Lost Lhasa" was first published in "Sandy Paws", an anthology about cats and dogs at the Delaware shore published by Cat & Mouse Press © 2020